ALL THAT SPARKLES

and shines

QUINN AVERY

For my dad - thank you for releasing my adventurous side by getting me hooked on the classics!

MYSTERY, SUSPENSE, & THRILLER

WRITTEN AS QUINN AVERY

www.QuinnAvery.com

BEXLEY SQUIRES MYSTERY SERIES

The Dead Girl's Stilettos

The Million Dollar Collar

The Guard's Last Watch

The Skeleton Key's Secrets

The Notebook's Hidden Truths

The Neighbor's Dark Past

STANDALONE ROMANTIC SUSPENSE/THRILLERS

What They Never Said

In Her Father's Shadow

Woman Over the Edge

Deadly Paradise

Lost Girls of Kato

Moscow Mules & Murder

Right Across the Bay

Their Little Lies

All That Sparkles & Shines

CHILDREN'S BOOKS

WRITTEN AS JENNIFER NAUMANN

bit.ly/dogsdonthavefins

Dogs Don't Have Fins

Dogs Don't Have Antlers

All That Sparkles & Shines
1st Edition

Cover: Best of You
ISBN: 979-8-9906697-1-0
Library of Congress Control Number: applied
www.QuinnAvery.com

CHAPTER 1
The Woman

NEARLY A DOZEN HOURS after the sun had set on what she would later realize had been the worst day of her life, the woman awoke on a bed of leaves inside a densely wooded forest to the sinister cry of a crow. The air was damp, and a deep inhale filled her with the sharp, tangy scent of earth and pine. Crisp, early morning rays of sunlight pierced through the fine pine needles over her head, casting the beginning of a spotlight onto her surroundings. Her head ached and throbbed with a ferocity that at first made it seem impossible to sit upright.

Her heart plummeted when she managed to prop herself onto her forearms. The tall Red Fir trees surrounding her stretched for countless miles without a single structure—or another human—in sight. The grand, jagged shadows of mountains loomed in the distance, seemingly not too far away to reach by foot.

Where was she?

Confusion settled over her brain with the intensity of a sudden thunderstorm on a perfectly sunny day. She had no memory of what she had been doing or how she arrived in such a breathtakingly beautiful yet terrifyingly desolate landscape. She would have to call…*someone* to come get her. When she couldn't recall a single name of anyone in her life, greasy panic swirled through her gut. She couldn't so much as conjure a familiar face—not even of the people who had raised her.

"Calm down," she groused under her breath. "You're just disoriented."

When she turned her head to look in the other direction, the sharp pain pressing against her skull made her cry out. She reached behind her skull, finding a sickly cool glob nestled inside her hair. When she brought her hand back for inspection, her fingers dusted with sediment were soaked with partially congealed blood. She glanced over at the ground behind her and found a small rock covered in more blood.

But discovering she was wounded didn't upset her as much as her subsequent discovery.

The feminine, slim fingers with a modest collection of silver rings and polish-free, naturally long fingernails were unfamiliar. She continued her examination, finding the slender arms and royal blue sweatshirt extending from the hand equally foreign. She bent to examine dirty blue jeans on athletic thighs and tan hiking boots with signs of extreme wear and tear. Long, golden hair framed her vision. She took a chunk of it between her fingers, deciding the deep waves and honey shade seemed natural as opposed to being something from a bottle. It was thick and healthy although in dire need of a good brushing.

Sharp tingles of unease spread down her spine. She was no longer concerned about the thick forest or the fact that she had no idea how to find her way out.

She was a stranger to herself.

Alarm bubbled inside her chest as she attempted slow, calming breaths. She somehow sensed she was intelligent, and was confident she could work everything out with time. She patted the jeans' front and back pockets, praying she'd discover either a cell phone or a driver's license. She'd settle for anything that would enlighten the situation. But the pockets were all empty.

She reached behind her, ready to push on the hard ground to stand. Her right hand came down on something cold and unyielding. Before she could turn around, her fingers had worked out the chilling details of the mystery object.

A gun.

More specifically, a 9 mm pistol.

"There's a reasonable explanation for this," she told herself, marveling her voice's low, silky tone. "Maybe you're a cop." Her eyes skittered across her casual clothing to the vast gathering of trees with skepticism. "Or a forest ranger," she amended.

As she recoiled from the weapon, something poked her left breast. *Please don't let it be a knife,* she thought as she hesitantly reached inside the lacy bra she was wearing. The discovery of a gun had been jarring enough.

Her breath caught when her fingers retrieved a dazzling blue jewel. It was nearly the size of a silver dollar, significantly heavy, and covered in a thick layer of red dirt. She licked her thumb and rubbed a side of the jewel clean, revealing its brilliance. Enough sparkle emitted that it seemed probable it was a genuine diamond.

Her lips puckered with a low whistle. "No *way* this is real," she decided. Something so flawless and vivid would be worth hundreds of thousands... maybe even *millions* if it were genuine. Bile rose in her throat with the next thought to cross her mind. *Maybe that's the reason she was carrying a pistol.* The excruciating pain in her skull was all at once accompanied by an intensive bout of nausea. *Was she a jewel thief?*

The persistent cawing of crows caught her attention. She turned to the sound, finding the pesky bastards a handful of yards away. They pecked at the ground, keeping their beady eyes on a figure nearby. Narrowing her gaze on their target, she realized she was looking at the soles of a pair of combat boots. Knowing someone was nearby—possibly also knocked out as she had clearly been—temporarily lifted her spirits.

Then she remembered the gun.

Had she been protecting herself from someone before she became unconscious? Was the man a threat? Had he hit her over the head?

She reached behind her back again, curling her fingers around the pistol's rough handle. She brought the weapon into her lap and studied it, hoping it would trigger a tangible memory. It felt surprisingly comfortable in her hand, adding to her suspicion that she might be some kind of officer of the law. *Or a skilled criminal,* her conscience nagged.

As she slowly pushed off the ground and rose on wobbly legs, the crows took flight, and the figure they'd been gathered around came into focus. With her heart slipping into her throat, she gripped the pistol against her thigh. A large man lay sprawled on his back, motionless. She guessed him to be in his mid to upper 60s. He possessed a husky frame and closely-cropped salt-and-pepper hair and wore cargo pants and a military jacket zipped over a black T-shirt. She guessed the coat was only a fashion statement and not an actual uniform issued by one of the armed forces. But she wasn't sure of anything in that moment.

Knots twisted through her gut as she shuffled closer in the fresh dirt. The hard lines of the man's aged face were as slack as his gaping mouth. Dark, glassy eyes stared at the trees overhead, unblinking. A pool of dried blood came from a bullet hole in his abdomen, visible through his clothing.

A surprised gasp fell over her lips. She squeezed her eyes shut, telling herself she was trapped in a nightmare. But when her eyelids flipped back open, the man was still there. Still dead.

There was no point in checking for a pulse. He'd clearly been dead for hours while she had laid blissfully unconscious nearby. She turned her head as her stomach upheaved, expelling God knows what onto the ground. Frantic thoughts wove through her pounding head as she leaned against the nearest tree.

A stranger was dead from a gunshot wound.

She was in possession of a pistol and a jewel with a potentially astronomical value.

She knew absolutely nothing about the situation.

She knew absolutely nothing about herself.

For all she knew, she was an escaped serial killer.

She may have been a stranger to herself, but she was certain she wasn't the type who would want to spend a single minute behind bars. There was clearly only one choice laid out before her.

She had to run.

By the time the first hint of civilization filled her vision, she was exhausted from trekking through the forest for countless hours. She wanted to cry tears of relief at the sight of the little town nestled among tall trees and distant mountains. Several small buildings painted in bright colors with whimsical fonts on the stores' signs lined a 2-lane road for three blocks before the town became peppered with small dwellings. It emitted a resort-like atmosphere, complete with dozens of tourists walking about, taking the scenery in with bright, curious eyes. Although some of her hoped to make contact with someone who could help her find her way home—wherever that may be—she was also afraid to interact with anyone. Who could she possibly trust at that point?

The pistol dug into her stomach as she wearily approached a window on the first building with "RESNER BREWERY" painted in a large, modern font on the brick facade over the industrial black windows. The trendy establishment featured edgy paintings and decor adorning the walls, live edge walnut tables, large steel drums of draft beer, and industrial stools facing a counter backed by schooners and growlers on open shelving. Patrons in their 20s and 30s formed a line leading to the counter and filled the tables, some deeply engaged in their open laptops and others chatting animatedly on their cell phones. Although her stomach growled angrily when spotting a mammoth-sized grilled sandwich and mac and cheese on a nearby patron's plate, she couldn't imagine she looked fit to enter the establishment. Besides, she hadn't found a single cent in her possession.

She kept her head down as she continued along the sidewalk that took her past a quaint bookstore, a handful of women's clothing boutiques, a hardware store, a cafe, and an antique store. At the end of the row of mom-and-pop businesses, men and women boarded a gray coach bus parked in the road. Behind them, a sign over a little white building read, BUS

SHOP & STOP. If only she'd been lucky enough to have found a billfold on her, it would've been an easy escape from what ever situation she was in. She casually passed a group of teenagers to peer inside the building's dusty windows. The station appeared to double as a convenience store, complete with basic groceries and souvenirs. Several shirts in the window display boasted CAVE JUNCTION, OR across the chest. She wasn't exactly surprised to learn she was in Oregon. But was it based on the scenery or because she was familiar with the town? She feared she might be a local and accordingly had to do something to alter her appearance as soon as possible.

A short, stout man scribbled on a white board beside the register. He had already written, *"Boarding has begun for San Diego"* and the woman watched in interest as he wrote beneath it, *"Astoria to begin boarding in two hours."*

Something about Astoria nagged in the back of the woman's mind. It was the first feeling of familiarity she'd experienced all day. Feeling hopeful, she swallowed past the dryness in her throat as she backed away from the building. She had two hours to make herself unrecognizable to anyone who might know her and find a way onto that bus.

CHAPTER 2

Brock

FROM THE BACK of the coach bus, Brock Resner watched with annoyance and curiosity as the athletic brunette climbed the stairway in front. Public transportation wasn't usually his thing. Still, he figured it wouldn't hurt to try experiencing Cave Junction as a bonafide tourist. And once he'd witnessed the delightfully curvy blonde swiping his credit card off the table at his brewery and using it to color her hair before purchasing a ticket, he was heavily invested in learning more about the attractive thief. He'd been impressed by her stealthy abilities and figured it was something she'd successfully done before. The amount she'd charged wasn't a concern as she was clearly in a bind, and the credit card company would cover it once he called to explain it had been stolen.

He continued to watch the young woman's every

move as she started down the aisle before selecting a seat two rows ahead of him. Dusty blue jeans nicely cupped her shapely backside, and the oversized Cave Junction sweatshirt did very little to hide her generous breasts. Her features were feminine and well-aligned, making her naturally beautiful without a trace of makeup. She'd dyed her voluminous hair a walnut brown and had trimmed it from her elbows to an inch or two past her shoulders. Brock's jeans involuntarily tightened as he imagined all that thick hair sprawled on his white sheets.

A cheap pair of convenience store sunglasses covered the woman's eyes as she kept her head down and clutched her only possession—the plain white bag from the bus stop where she must've used his card to purchase the sunglasses and sweatshirt—close to her chest. She was clearly afraid of something or someone. Brock intended to find out what or who.

As he imagined she'd been watching him closely before she'd found an opportunity to swipe his card, he'd grabbed one of the baseball hats his brewery sold to cover his mop of brown curls and stuffed the bright red sweatshirt he'd been wearing into his overnight bag.

Before long, the driver closed the door, and the bus was in motion. The seats were less than half full, allowing the woman to stretch out before leaning her head against the window. She didn't appear to move over the next several hours. Once she woke and used the restroom before returning to her seat, Brock grabbed the bottles of water and package of beef jerky he'd purchased before boarding the bus and slipped into the seat next to the woman. She was curled up against the window, sunglasses propped on her head, eyes closed. In addition to smelling earthy, her blue jeans and hiking boots were dusted with dirt. He noticed a faint cluster of freckles across the bridge of her pixie-like nose and quickly decided she was even more alluring up close.

Before her eyes opened, she leaned into him and jabbed something sharp against his side. "Who are you?" she demanded in a sultry voice.

He stifled the chuckle tickling against his throat. "Although the dark hair emits some sexy Angelina Jolie vibes, I still prefer you as a blonde."

"What do you want?"

"I *want* my credit card back," he scoffed.

Eyes the color of vibrant grass in the springtime widened on him before she backed away and slipped whatever weapon she'd used back into her pocket. "I cut it up, disposed of it in the gas station garbage." Scraping her teeth over her thick bottom lip, she glanced across the aisle to the empty seats nearby.

"I'm sorry. If you give me your address, I'll pay you back…somehow. Every cent."

"Damn right, you will." He held out the open bag of jerky between them. "Don't be shy. I know you already had a sandwich on my dime, but that was hours ago."

The woman's skittish gaze jumped to the jerky before returning to narrow on him. "Are you going to call the police?"

He lifted a shoulder. "Depends on whether or not you have a good reason to steal from me."

Her slender fingers dug into the plastic bag still in her lap as she looked away. "I'm…trying to get away from someone."

"I figured as much by the hasty makeover." When she refused the jerky, he dropped the bag in his lap and deposited one of the waters onto the seat by her hip. "From the cops or someone else?"

Hesitating for a moment, she nibbled on her bottom lip. "Someone else."

"Husband?" He glanced down at her left hand, finding it ring-free. "Boyfriend?"

She answered with a tiny nod.

He flexed his jaw. "What's your plan once you get to Astoria?"

A deep sigh fell from her pretty little lips. "I

haven't thought that far ahead. I don't know where I'm going."

"What about friends or family?"

A wistful look passed over her features. "There's…no one."

Brock removed the baseball cap and scratched at his wayward curls. It was in his DNA to help a woman running from an abusive relationship, as his mom had worked at a family shelter when he was young. It didn't hurt that this woman happened to be hot, although now he wouldn't be acting on his attraction to her because of her situation. He had to admit he was a little disappointed. "I'm short a bartender at my brewery in Astoria. You can work off what you owe me instead of hourly pay and live off your tips until the debt's paid. There's an empty apartment above the brewery that you're welcome to use until you decide your next move."

"I-I'm not sure bartending is in my skill set," she stuttered.

"You'll learn." He eyed her death grip on the bag. "You didn't grab any of your things before you left?"

"There wasn't time to think it through. I just had to get out of there."

"You look close to the same size as my sister," he told her. Although he suspected Skye was several sizes beyond the petite thief, his sister would undoubtedly empathize with someone in a similar situation Skye had found herself in not too long ago. "I'm sure she can loan you some stuff until you get back on your feet."

"Why are you being so nice to me after what I did?" When her vivid green eyes swept over his face, Brock was sure he detected a bit of mutual desire. Especially once her cheeks flushed. "What is it you're expecting in return?"

"Loyalty as one of my employees. Nothing more and nothing less." He offered his hand. "Brock Resner."

Glancing at his ball cap, the woman's golden complexion paled once she realized that he'd been a patron in his own brewery when she'd taken his card. "I'm not…I mean, I can't—"

"It's okay to make something up," he interrupted with a hint of a smile. "Nothing about this job offer is typical anyway. It's not like I'll run a background check and ask for references. I'm merely putting blind faith in someone who could use a little help."

"It's Andy," she blurted, immediately appearing to regret the disclosure by the way she winced. "Andy…Fratelli?"

"You're offering your name as a question?" he teased. When she still looked unsure of herself, he laughed. "Sounds legit enough to me." He nudged her hand until she finally accepted his handshake. "Nice to meet you, Andy Fratelli. I mean, despite the unusual circumstances and everything."

Her hand inside his felt warm, her grip stronger than he'd been expecting. He acknowledged it wasn't wise to employ someone who had proved themselves dishonest but someone had to give the woman a break. Who knew what kind of monster she was running from?

Andy's gaze traveled over the studio apartment's exposed brick walls, the small kitchenette with stainless steel appliances, the tan leather couch paired with a barn wood coffee table, the flatscreen hanging across from the sofa, and what could be seen of the bathroom with the door only slightly ajar. Lastly, she focused on the steel stairway to the queen bed lofted beneath the industrial windows. Brock had lived in the efficient space for almost a full year during the construction of his new home overlooking the Astoria-Megler Bridge. He'd since only used the apartment a few times for hookups with tourists he'd met in the brewery and, most recently, a match on his app who'd garnered his interest for several months before he realized she was batshit crazy. Thankfully, his maid had stopped by to wash the bedding since his final conquest with Christina, erasing any lingering trace of the psychopath.

The idea of dirtying the sheets with Andy stirred another strong tug of desire as he watched her take it all in. Although muscular, she was as short and petite as a 13-year-old with all the mouth-watering curves of a grown woman. If he had to guess, she was around his age or even a few years younger. Everything about her made him want to claim her with an intense need he hadn't felt in a long time.

"It's not much," he told her, "but it's clean. It's all yours as long as you keep working for me."

"Looks expensive." She turned to him with doubt heavy in her gaze. "How long will it take me to repay you for staying here?"

"You only owe the amount you charged to my card. This place sits empty anyway. I've never thought to rent it out." He pulled his phone out of his back pocket to find a message from his sister. "Skye's on her way with some clothes and necessities. She should be here in ten minutes or so. I didn't know your shoe size, so she grabbed several pairs of sneakers from her boutique. You're going to need a good pair for bartending. We'll hook you up with one of the brewery's T-shirts when you check in for your first shift." He handed her the key to the apartment.

"You start tomorrow at noon. I'll come in to train you for a week or two until you're comfortable."

"This is all too much," Andy declared with an exasperated sigh. "I can't just accept everything you're offering when I don't know how long I'll stay in Astoria."

"At least long enough to pay your debt." He held her gaze with a long, hard look to let her know he meant business. It may have been overly generous, but he could afford to give her whatever she needed ten times over. Besides, he enjoyed using his wealth for good. He opened the front door, turning back to give Andy a friendly smile. "See you tomorrow."

He chided himself on the way back down to where he'd parked his Tesla in the street behind the brewery and paced while waiting for his sister. Although he'd created a wildly popular way for people to meet up online, his sex life had become stale after he'd invested his millions into creating a franchise of equally successful breweries. Every minute of his free time was spent nurturing his legacy. While he had no business lusting after Andy Fratelli or whoever she may be, he couldn't seem to help himself.

CHAPTER 3

Andy

THE MOMENT the apartment door closed behind Brock, "Andy Fratelli" raced up to the loft and stuffed the pistol under the mattress. She frantically searched every square inch available for a foolproof place to hide the blue diamond. Inside the tiny bathroom, she pushed on the paneled ceiling and discovered a secure ledge where the grid system met a handful of studs. After she carefully set the diamond on the ledge and lowered the ceiling panel back into place, she studied the stranger's reflection in the mirror hung over the vanity.

The green-eyed woman staring back at her could've been anywhere from twenty-one to thirty-three, but she sensed she was older than twenty-something. She was pretty enough with a healthy glow from many hours spent in the sunshine and big round eyes that made her stand out. Although she was no closer to learning her identity, she had at least discovered without question that she was attracted to men.

From the moment Brock had claimed the open seat beside her on the bus, and she'd heard his husky voice, her pulse had thudded with excitement beneath her skin. With a broad jaw, perfect teeth, a slightly hooked nose, unruly brown hair that curled past his ears, and youthful brown eyes that emitted warmth no matter his mood, Brock was boyishly handsome. She'd taken her time in appreciating his broad shoulders and muscular arms while he'd napped in the aisle across from her. And when she'd followed him off the bus, it was impossible not to admire how his jeans hugged his tight rear.

She'd been shocked by how quickly she'd defended herself with the bottle opener she'd added to her other purchases on a whim. The offer to work at his brewery and stay in the apartment had been even more of a shock. She wasn't convinced she knew the first thing about bartending, and she was afraid someone six hours north of Cave Junction could still recognize her.

Because of her situation, she would've been crazy to turn him down. She knew no one, and she had nothing. Where else would she have gone? Yet she couldn't help feeling massive guilt for accepting his generosity when she most likely didn't deserve it. If nothing else, she'd lied to him about being a victim. At least between the festering guilt and the failed attempt as a petty thief, she was starting to believe she wouldn't have shot the man in the forest without a valid reason. She only hoped that reason didn't involve her stealing the precious gem she'd safely tucked away.

With a knock on the apartment's front door, her heart stilled. How could she be sure it was Brock's sister, and not someone who'd followed her from Cave Junction? She reluctantly started for the door and peered through the peephole.

The woman standing in the hallway was as attractive as her brother, and had same wild brown locks and warm brown eyes. She was also close to her brother's height, towering over Andy by at least a foot. In ripped jeans, a Stevie Nicks T-shirt under a leather jacket, hair pulled back in a complicated braid that wove around her narrow head, dozens of ear piercings, and scuff-free Adidas, Andy guessed the woman was a trendy, free spirit.

When Andy opened the door, Skye gave her an enduring grin that exposed blindingly white teeth. "You must be Andy!" she exclaimed, stepping inside.

Andy cringed at the sound of her bogus name. At

first, she worried her memory had returned, and she'd disclosed her real name to Brock. Once she realized she'd created it based on characters from *The Goonies,* a film she discovered she could recite in her head nearly line-for-line, it was too late to take it back. It was unfair she could remember trivial things like a movie script yet still couldn't glean any facts about herself. She also found it quite ironic that she'd taken a bus to the very location of said movie. Maybe her decision to come to Astoria hadn't been serendipitous.

"I'm Skye…Brock's big sister." She held up both arms adorned with half a dozen reusable shopping bags. "I brought a few things to get you through your first shift. Tomorrow night, you can come by my shop to pick out some fun, casual outfits."

Andy tugged on the neckline of the sweatshirt she'd purchased in Cave Junction. "You didn't have to go to all this trouble. I can get by with what I have."

Skye laughed in a bubbly sound as she breezed in past Andy. "No offense, sister, but those old boots and jeans won't get you the big tips." She set the bags on the coffee table and began digging inside one. "My brother did a great job of guessing your pants size. Considering how many women he's pampered over the years, I suppose it shouldn't be a surprise."

Andy felt an unwarranted pang of jealousy. It shouldn't surprise her that Brock was a ladies' man. In addition to being handsome, she suspected he was quite wealthy based on his multiple breweries and expensive car.

Skye produced a pair of ripped jeans similar to her own and held them up for Andy to inspect. "What do you think of these? Are they your style?"

Andy held in a sudden burst of laughter. Other than the outfit she'd been wearing in the forest, she didn't know a thing about her preference of clothing. "They'll do," she decided without a hint of enthusiasm.

"I grabbed you several undergarments to choose from, too." Skye stuffed the jeans back where they came from before handing the entire bag over. "I'm sure you're dying to clean up after the day you've had. I'm just going to leave everything here on the table. Keep whatever pair of shoes you like, and bring the rest when you stop to see me tomorrow. The store will be closed by the time your shift is over, but I'll still be there doing inventory. It's located in the next building down from here—Skye's Unlimited." Her eyes widened. "Oh! I grabbed a disposable phone while shopping for everything else you'll need—shampoo, deodorant, some water and snacks, etcetera. I already programmed my number and

Brock's into the phone. Neither of us lives too far away, so don't hesitate to call if you need anything." She placed a hand on Andy's shoulder. "It's safe to use, Andy. No one will be able to trace it back to you."

Overwhelmed by her generosity, Andy briefly considered telling Skye the truth and asking for her help. She sensed Skye would empathize with her dilemma and help her dig for answers. Then again, the truth could place the kind brother and sister in danger. Andy couldn't live with herself if anything happened to either of them. It was best to keep them both blissfully unaware of her confusing situation.

She leaned in to wrap her arms around Skye. "Thank you."

Skye embraced her back in a firm hold. "Everything will be okay."

Andy doubted that was true.

"Be a good girl while I'm gone," a husky voice whispered in her ear as a set of arms squeezed her too tightly. It hurt. She couldn't draw in a breath. As she stared at the massive rock in the water, the arms tightened even more. "No matter what people say about me…no matter what you hear…I will always love you. Always and forever."

• • •

Heart hammering, Andy blinked rapidly against the darkness. Had the dream been a product of her imagination, or were her memories beginning to return?

After a heavy night's sleep that included a more detailed dream involving her and Brock doing erotic things to each other, Andy flushed when her new employer's eyes met hers as she entered Resner Brewery ten minutes before noon. Her belly warmed under his milk chocolate stare. *Those eyes.* They were enigmatic and inviting simultaneously, piercing a hole right through her. He seemed incapable of hiding his feelings or knowing he was regarding her like a starved man would eye an endless buffet. She vowed not to let herself get involved with him or anyone else as long as her life was a complete mystery.

She broke his gaze to survey the building. The vibe was similar to the brewery in Cave Junction, only twice as large with industrial-height ceilings rather than standard height. Two teenage girls stood close to each other at the other end of the brewery, frantically whispering. Andy sensed she had always despised female drama and made a mental note not to give her coworkers anything to conspire about.

"You're early," Brock announced as she approached where he stood behind the register. A sexy grin tugged at his agreeable lips. "I'll chalk it up as one of your redeeming factors." His eyes roamed over the sneakers and ripped jeans Skye had brought the night before, the sweatshirt Andy had purchased in Cave Junction, and settled on her stubby ponytail. "You look good today—er…I mean, well rested. Did Skye bring everything you needed?"

"And then some. She was extremely generous and told me to stop by her shop to pick out more outfits when I'm done here. Just so you know, I plan on paying her back, too."

"You can try, but she won't accept your money." The two waitresses broke into laughter across the room, and Brock rolled his eyes. "I'm having a hard time finding anyone over eighteen to work here. Ignore them, they're harmless. They're good kids but always gossiping and giggling about something." He crouched beneath the register, producing a ball cap and a folded black T-shirt with the same logo as the snug-fitting T-shirt he wore with a pair of black jeans. "I guess this is the only shirt we have left in stock. If it doesn't fit right, more should be coming next week."

Andy quickly averted her eyes away from his firm biceps as she snagged the shirt and cap from his grip. "I'm sure it'll be fine." She then gestured toward the "restrooms" sign. "I'll go change."

"When you're done, you can join me in my office. It's the door right next to the women's room. You can't miss it."

As she made her way to the ladies' room, her heart skipped a beat when she fully registered the extent of her commitment. How long until someone saw through her facade and learned the truth? Brock told her he wouldn't ask for references, but what if he needed her information for tax purposes? With several deep breaths, she convinced herself it was too early to panic.

Adjusting her hair around the opening of the ball cap, carefully avoiding the wound the ponytail was covering, she recalled how much blood had gone down the shower drain the night before. She sensed she should've had stitches and hoped, at the very least, she could avoid an infection. She slipped into the small T-shirt, amazed at how perfectly it fit despite being tight across her decently-endowed chest. A little healthy dose of cleavage could definitely increase her tips.

She exited the restroom, feeling optimistic for the first time since waking in the forest. Before going to bed, she'd used the incognito browsing mode on the basic smartphone from Skye to search for anything about a body found in the Josephine County forest. With a sense of dread, she realized the man could either rot for weeks before he was discovered or wild animals could wipe out any trace of his existence. While she obviously didn't want anything to trigger a search for her involvement with the man, she had also hoped his identity could shed some light on who *she* was and what she'd been doing in that forest.

As she entered the open door to Brock's sleek office, her heart leaped into her throat with the stark realization that she was done hiding.

They'd found her.

An intimidatingly broad-chested police officer in full uniform stood in the center of the room, his eyes growing impossibly wide on Andy as she breached the doorway.

CHAPTER 4

Brock

BROCK REALIZED his mistake when Andy braced herself against the doorway, appearing ready to collapse. Despite everything he'd said, she must've assumed he'd decided to turn her in. What if she'd physically harmed her boyfriend when defending herself? It would explain her skittish behavior. Worse yet, what if her boyfriend was the type that would make up a story to convince the cops to haul her back home? Brock should've been more conscious of the bad timing when his oldest friend knocked on the door.

Danny Knoxville was more of a brother than a friend. Brock had met him when they were in preschool, and they'd been inseparable since, save for the four years Brock spent at Iowa State, getting a degree in computer engineering and Knox was deployed overseas while serving in the Marine Corp. Still, they kept in touch throughout those years as much as their schedules would allow. Their mothers teasingly referred to them as "the twins" in high school—not because they had any physical resemblance to each other, but because they were never far apart. Knox was a blond-haired gym rat with the hulking muscles to prove it. Brock kept in shape by running and occasionally lifting weights, so he was long and lean, with a few inches of height on his oldest friend.

"Do I know you?" Knox asked Andy in a strange, unreadable tone.

She took a step back, appearing spooked. "Doubt it. I'm not from around here."

With a grunt, Knox scratched his fingers through the thick blond hair on the top of his head. It'd almost been a decade since he finished his time in the service, and he still closely shaved the sides. "I swear you look familiar."

Brock swallowed the lump rising in his throat. Based on his buddy's wide-eyed expression and hesitant stance, Brock feared Knox might've seen her on a wanted poster. "Andy, this is my buddy, Knox," he quickly explained, stepping between them. "He stops by occasionally to try and convince me to give him a free growler whenever he gets a bad match on my app."

Knox's eyes and shoulders both relaxed when he laughed. "That's because your app sucks," he sniggered, hooking his thumbs inside his utility belt and winking in Andy's direction. "If I were the investors, I'd demand a refund."

Andy tilted her head at Brock with one eyebrow raised. "Your app?"

Grunting under his breath, Brock flexed his jaw. He'd been in such a hurry to convince her that everything was alright that he'd broken his newest cardinal rule not to disclose the source of his wealth to a woman he was interested in getting to know on an intimate level. He seemed to have lost all focus when he'd noticed the T-shirt he'd given her was skin-tight against her breasts. He felt a misplaced surge of jealousy, figuring Knox would actively pursue the hot brunette now that they'd been introduced.

"You mean my boy didn't tell you?" Knox asked, slapping Brock's chest several times. "This genius right here is filthy rich. He's the man behind the Love Hive app. Sold his soul to the Silicon Valley gods when he was barely out of diapers. The fact that he's hanging out in one of his *many* investments, playing boss on a Saturday afternoon when he could be sailing around the world on a million-dollar yacht speaks volumes about his work ethic."

Had they been alone, Brock would've slugged Knox. He was well aware of Brock's hesitancy with women after the disaster with Christina. Brock feared his buddy was only harassing him because he could sense Brock's growing fascination with the mysterious woman. If that were the case, Brock was screwed. For all he knew, Andy was sue-happy and would file a sexual harassment case. And anyway, her character was still under question. Aside from showing up for her shift a handful of minutes early, the conniving little thief had yet to redeem herself.

"What brings you to Astoria?" Knox asked her.

"Gainful employment." Her seemingly forced smile softened as she turned away from him to address Brock. "I'm going to go introduce myself to the other waitresses."

Knox eyed her thoughtfully. "Nice meeting you… ah…I'm sorry, what was your name again?"

"Andy," Brock wheezed through clenched teeth.

"Andy," Knox repeated as she disappeared out of sight. He then turned to Brock and let out a low whistle. "Wow. She's *hot*. Guess now I understand why you can't go out with me tonight, you dirty bastard. I'd ice you out too if I had my sights set on a woman that sweet."

"She's my new employee," Brock snapped. "You can't joke about shit like that."

"Afraid she'll *sue* you for wanting to hook up? In her case, it'd be worth the expense." His eyes narrowed. "Where'd you meet her?"

"On the bus coming back from Cave Junction." Brock lowered into the leather chair behind the live oak desk custom-made along with the tables inside the restaurant. "She mentioned she was looking for work in Astoria, so I offered her a job. I've had a helluva time finding someone old enough to tend the bar so I don't have to be here every night." Although he was normally candid with Knox, he wasn't about to disclose the sordid details behind Andy's reason for fleeing to Astoria, especially not to someone sworn to uphold the law.

"Hold on." Knox lifted the palm on one hand. "You offered her a job on the spot?" His thick eyebrows shot up to his hairline as amusement twitched over his pale lips. "And did you say you took *a bus*?"

"I saw Andy buy a ticket, and I was intrigued. I hadn't booked a flight back, so I figured why not."

"You're saying you've resorted to stalking women?" Knox teased. "What's her story?"

Brock leaned back, tucking one side of his hair behind his ear. "Don't really know."

"You really are smitten with this woman, Resner. You followed a stranger onto a bus and agreed to give her free access to your business. Are you insane?" As Knox shook his head, his teasing smile faded away. "Want me to run a background check on her to ensure she's not some scam artist after your fortune?"

Brock briefly considered the offer. It would've been an elaborate scam, stealing his credit card to get close and assuming Brock wouldn't call the police. Besides, it seemed she couldn't have cared less when Knox mentioned his degree of wealth. Considering he was 99% certain she had given him a fictitious name based on characters in the popular 1980s film that put Astoria on the map, he stood by his vow to give her a chance when it seemed she had no one else. Besides, he wasn't entirely convinced that Andy was on the run because she had done something to her boyfriend—even if it had been in self-defense.

"Her credentials and references checked out," Brock lied. "Save your conspiracy theories for another day, Officer."

"If you say so." Knox gazed out the doorway and chuckled. "Now that I think about it, as much time as I spend down in Cave Junction, it's possible she's a past hookup from a drunken night."

The hand radio strapped to his chest beeped

before a monotone voice announced an officer was needed on scene for a code 10-57. Knox let out a heavy sigh. "Suppose I better answer that." His clear blue eyes flickered to the door before landing back on Brock. "Let me know if you change your mind about that background check."

"I won't," Brock assured him in a tone that came out harder than he intended.

To Brock's disappointment, Andy mastered her job within three days of arriving in Astoria and no longer needed his guidance. She was organized and efficient, shortening the wait time for drinks and training the teenage girls to take several tables' orders at once before retrieving drinks from the bar. Both the live edge bar and plank floor were spotless at all times, and she expertly mixed drinks that brought locals back for more. She'd even taught the other girls how to key in shortcuts when entering orders into the digital tablets—a feat that Brock, despite a degree in computer engineering, had been unable to achieve himself.

Over the next several weeks, he tried finding new ways to validate his lingering presence at the brewery. Sometimes, he surfed the internet from one of the tables, and sometimes, he helped out in the kitchen while secretly watching Andy. She practically danced from space to space, throwing charming smiles to customers and appropriately laughing at their attempted humor. She was kind to everyone and made fast friends with every last employee. Every day she reported to work in one of the few uniform T-shirts he'd given her with jeans from Skye and one of those crazy bun-thingies piled on top of her head. His fingers itched to yank the tie free and pull her close to taste her lips while losing his hands in her luscious locks. With every shift of her hips and curve of her delightful mouth, his pulse throbbed, and heat spread through his groin.

He was embarrassed to admit to anyone that there was literally nothing to keep him occupied once Andy no longer depended on him. He could've conducted business at the brewery he'd recently opened in Spokane, but he didn't want to leave Andy. He told himself it was because he was worried for her safety, but that was a blatant lie. He tried spending more time with Jane, his trusted book-keeper who came in three times weekly to pay invoices and deal with payroll, but she kicked him out within an hour. At least Knox came by more often than usual, proving a valid distraction. But he continued to watch Andy like he was trying to place her, making Brock uncomfortable and paranoid on her behalf.

As far as Brock could tell, Andy kept to herself outside work. Skye had invited herself to the apartment a few times with a bottle of wine and reported that Andy was friendly but still reserved. He was determined to get to know her better in every way imaginable.

One night around closing time, almost exactly two months into her employment with him, he caught an interaction between Andy and a 30-something male tourist seated at a table with a group of similarly aged buddies. The man's eyes were on Andy's chest as he spoke to her, and her face wrenched with discomfort as she took a step back. Brock started for them, intending to kick the creeper out.

"I'm sorry, I don't have time to date," she said to the man, her voice clipped with irritation.

"Who said anything about dating, sweetheart?" With a sickening grin, the man reached out to cup Andy's backside. "I just want a little taste of this sweet ass."

Rage gripped Brock's spine as he charged toward them. He wasn't normally a violent man, but he felt a primal urge to knock the prick right off his stool. Before he reached them, however, Andy spun around, grabbing the man's arm and violently pinning it behind his back.

"I'm going to let you in on a little secret," she growled threateningly. "Women don't appreciate being groped by sleazy perverts." She yanked his arm a little higher, causing him to cry out in pain. "Touch me again, and you'll wake in the ER with a tube jammed down your throat so you can breathe."

"I'm sorry!" The man winced, leaning into her grip. "I won't do it again!"

"Damn right you won't," Brock snarled at him, pointing to the exit. The urge to punch the guy's lights out still warmed his blood. "Pay your bill and leave a generous tip, then get the hell out. I don't ever want to see you in here again."

Their stools scraped against the hardwood floor as the four men rose from the table and hurriedly reached for their wallets. Brock stood watching them until they had paid and exited as directed. He turned to Andy once they were gone, wishing he could pull her into his arms. "You alright?"

"I'm sorry, I shouldn't have done that," she muttered as she collected the money the men had left behind. "I don't know what got into me."

"You serious? You should've just broken that asshole's arm. Guys like that need to be taught a lesson." *Guys like the boyfriend she'd run away from,* he silently added. Had she tried standing up to him, too? The way she quickly cleaned the table, breathing heavily through her mouth, he decided she was pretty shaken up from the incident. "Why don't you go ahead and close out whatever tables you still have open, then join me for a beer? You look like you could use one."

Her shoulders fell when she met his gaze. "I think I could go for something stronger."

"Whatever you want—it's on the house."

She gave him a tentative smile. "Thanks, Brock."

As she walked away, he decided he was even more interested in hearing her story. He was dying to know what exactly went down with her boyfriend before she'd left Cave Junction.

CHAPTER 5

Andy

AFTER CONFRONTING THE PERVERT, Andy's insides trembled. Once again, she was unnerved by her aggressive nature. Who *was* she? Why did it feel so natural to react with violence? Every night after work, she browsed the internet for anything about a missing woman or a dead man near Cave Junction, hoping for the slightest clue as to the truth. If she had a family, they must've been frantic by that point, yet no one came looking. Her situation felt more hopeless than ever when she considered there might not be anyone who cared about her whereabouts.

She'd become comfortable in Astoria. Having a steady job and a safe place to go at night made her feel normal, despite still not knowing her name or what she was doing with a gun and a rare gem. The dream in which she was told to be a good girl had returned several times, reminding her she knew absolutely nothing about who she was or where she'd come from. And too often, she'd experience the creeping sensation of someone watching her.

Since there was no way to know whether or not she was safe, she didn't stray far from the brewery or the apartment except for late-night runs through town. It felt natural to stay in shape, so she'd started a routine that involving high protein meals, cardio exercises, and lifting heavy items around the apartment instead of weights.

Although she enjoyed bartending and had become friendly with her teenage coworkers, her favorite part about working there was spending every day with Brock. The other girls had commented on several occasions that it was weird having him around all the time, and more than once, she'd caught him playing games on his laptop rather than "working," as he always claimed. She couldn't decide if he was purposely keeping an eye on her because he still didn't trust her or was worried for her safety. Either way, she had to admit she was grateful he stuck around.

As for Brock's buddy, the police officer, she

wasn't sure how she felt about him always stopping by, even when he wasn't in uniform. The way she sometimes caught Knox looking at her, she worried he was only waiting for to ask her out. She unquestionably wasn't interested in getting involved with an officer of the law.

As Brock mixed two margaritas behind the bar following the groping incident, she couldn't help but admire the way his biceps flexed and his chest slightly bulged beneath his T-shirt. Although she was still convinced it was a bad idea to act on her attraction toward him, his constant presence made her feel a little less forlorn.

Once their drinks were made, he handed her one of the highball glasses and slipped onto the stool at her side. "Cheers."

They clinked glasses before she took a long swig. The ache in her feet and back instantly eased a little with the sour mixer and strong liquor, but her nerves remained on edge. For the first time since arriving in Astoria, she was convinced she could be someone dangerous.

"Since you have the day off tomorrow, I thought maybe you'd wanna join me for a stroll on the Riverwalk Trail," Brock said, swirling the ice in his glass. "It's a great way to see the city and check out some of the local businesses."

She paused to consider his offer. She sensed she couldn't fight her growing attraction toward him forever, but she owed it to him to try. And although being on a public trail seemed safe enough so long as she wore her brewery ball cap and avoided eye contact with others, she still worried Brock would get caught in the crossfire if things went south. Besides, she had planned to spend her day off at the library, researching rare gems the old-school way so as not to leave a digital thumbprint. The incognito search mode on the burner phone wasn't foolproof and could alert the wrong kind of people to her location. "I'm busy."

His brown eyebrows winged upward. "All day?"

She ran her fingers along the icy glass and eyed him with suspicion. "You realize you're probably only single because you're already married to this place, right? If what your buddy said was true about you being filthy rich, why do you spend so much time here among us peasants? Why not travel the world or save some endangered species?"

He grunted while swallowing his drink. "I like to keep a close eye on my investments."

"By your investments, you mean me."

Turning to her, his lips tilted with a crooked grin. "Can you blame me? You're only here because you stole my credit card."

"I get the feeling that's not the only reason you're keeping a close eye on me." She took another sip of the sour drink before regarding him once more. "What's your game, Resner? Your sister mentioned I'm not the first woman you've tried to pamper. Am I your little pet project of the month? Do you plan to play with me for a while, then move on to the next attractive employee to catch your eye?"

A look of genuine alarm passed through his expression. "Why would you think that?"

"Rich, good-looking men are usually single for a good reason. Either their ego's too big to commit to one woman, or they bore easily."

"I'm *not* a player," he insisted, his tone crisp. "I don't play games with women."

She leaned into him, eyes sliding over his well-proportioned features. "Are you going to deny you want to hook up with me?"

"I'm your boss."

She drew back and let out a dubious hum. By the rushed way he uttered the words, it seemed he was only trying to convince himself. "That doesn't answer my question."

"It does if I don't want to get sued for sexual harassment."

"You don't have to worry about that happening

with me. But I'm not sure how much longer I'll be in Astoria. Once my debt to you is paid—"

"It was paid off weeks ago," he assured her. "You'll be getting a chunk of cash in a few days. But I'm really hoping you'll decide to stay anyway. I'd really like the chance to get to know you better."

Quietly laughing, she wished she could get to know herself better, too. "You might change your mind once that happens." She chugged the remainder of her margarita before setting the empty glass down on the bar top. "Thanks for the drink. I'm going to head up to the apartment for the night."

He gave her a reluctant look, almost as if contemplating inviting himself to join her. She could feel their unspoken desires for one another crackling between them. "Are you sure you don't want to join me on the Riverwalk tomorrow?"

"Good night, Brock," she replied, walking away.

She knew she was being coldhearted, but it was best for both of them if their relationship remained platonic.

By the time Andy returned to work after a solid day of researching at the library, her head was swimming with information regarding cut, color, clarity, and carat weight, in addition to faint and fancy hues, levels of boron, and the history of mining. More certain than before that she had one of the rarest gems in the world, she was jumpy and on edge with every new customer to enter the brewery. When she felt a hand on her shoulder while pouring a frothy ale, she whirled around in preparation to strike her attacker, sending the half-full glass down to shatter on the floor.

Meghan, one of her coworkers, was quick to help her mop up the mess with bar rags. "Oh my god, Andy, I'm so sorry! I didn't mean to scare you!"

Meghan was an honors student recently nominated the high school's homecoming queen. She was Andy's favorite person to work alongside. Meghan was genuinely friendly and had an easygoing smile. She'd been dating the homecoming king for three years, so she wasn't into gossiping about boys as much as the others. Still, men of all ages relentlessly hit on her. Her honey-blond hair, worn in quirky styles without fail, shone with a healthy glow that matched the glimmer of her sharp cheekbones and the sparkle in her wide, cornflower eyes. She was the type of flawless beauty they modeled Barbie dolls after.

"It's all good," Andy assured her, pressing a clean

rag against her damp T-shirt. "I guess I'm a little out of it today."

Meghan's thick lashes fluttered with concern. "Is everything alright?"

Andy threw her a warm smile. "I'm fine, Meghan."

"Good, because I came over here to invite you to a party at our house tonight." She flashed Andy an equally inviting smile. "It's kind of formal—my dad's the District Attorney, and he's throwing a birthday bash for some big wig from the Coast Guard. But you don't have to dress too fancy if you don't feel like it. I know you don't have a car, but it's within walking distance, down a few blocks on Ninth Street…the massive red house with a wraparound porch and several turrets. You can't miss it."

"I'm not much of a party gal," Andy told her. "I prefer staying in."

"That's exactly why I'm inviting you. You've been here for a hot minute already, and don't know anyone outside this place. It would do you good to mingle…meet some locals." Grinning devilishly, she twirled a lock of her golden hair through her fingers. "*Brock* is going to be there."

With a steady expression, Andy resumed pouring the ale. "Why would I care if our boss is going to be there?"

"Oh, come on," Meghan teased with a tongue click. "We've *all* seen how you look at each other. There's nothing wrong with two single, crazy-hot adults hooking up. It's like the two of you were meant for each other. Besides, it wouldn't matter what you're doing together if it one day leads to *marriage*. Then you could be my boss, too!"

With the mention of marriage, Andy nearly dropped the glass again. For all she knew, she was already married. "Seriously, Meghan, you need to get your head out of the clouds and stop watching the Hallmark Channel. This isn't some feel-good romcom in which the hometown millionaire hooks up with a bartender on the run."

Meghan giggled with her head tilted. "What would *you* be on-the-run from?"

Andy's pulse thrummed a little faster. "Isn't that normally what happens in those sappy love stories? The woman is down-on-her-luck and looking for a man to save her?" Laughing brightly, she finished pouring the drink and reached for a second glass. "I can promise you, my problems aren't something that can be solved by a handsome alpha male with a fat stack of cash."

"Whatever. I never said anything about him *saving* you, Andy. I just though you'd be cute together…and maybe someday have gorgeous babies. Besides, you could make your own fat stack of cash by becoming an influencer. I bet some makeup company out there would kill to use your eyes for their brand."

"I think that should be *your* move," Andy said, handing her the two full glasses. "It'd probably pay for your tuition at Berkley."

"I wish," Meghan muttered, glancing down at the pilsner glasses in her hands. "Maybe then my dad would get off my back for a change."

"What could he possibly have to complain about with you?"

"You'd be surprised." Meghan lifted the glasses. "I better get these to that rowdy table of frat boys. I don't want to give them anything else to harass me about."

"Don't let men mess with you like that," Andy warned. "Once they see you as weak and defenseless, they'll become even more relentless. Stand up to them—let them know you're strong and won't put up with their shit."

A light shone in Meghan's beautiful blue eyes when she nodded. "I'll remember that."

Andy's heart sank as the teenager left her. She would've loved to have gotten dressed up for a party and had the chance to meet more people. She yearned to become a part of something, especially a community. If her memory didn't return soon, she didn't know what she would do. But one thing was certain—she didn't have the strength to isolate herself from genuine relationships and the outside world for much longer.

CHAPTER 6

Brock

DRESSED in a tan jacket paired with a white dress shirt, navy trousers, and suede penny loafers, Brock climbed the stairway leading up to the District Attorney's historic mansion. He hesitated before reaching for the large set of door handles, cocking his head to listen as loud jazz music and the lively din of conversation oozed from the house. Parties and mingling weren't his thing. He usually only endured them if it was an event for a noble cause. But Meghan had mentioned Andy was invited, and he was eager for a chance to spend time with her outside of the brewery.

Once he'd mustered the courage to insert himself into the madness, the door opened on its own. His stomach lurched with the sight of the curvaceous blonde in the striking red dress beaming back at him. Had they been attending a Marilyn Monroe contest, she would've been guaranteed to win.

"Brock, babe! I can't believe you're here!" Christina, his last girlfriend who'd done everything short of stabbing him in his sleep after they'd broken up, leaped toward him, throwing her arms around his neck. "I've missed you so much!"

The familiar scent of her rose perfume released a flurry of cringe-worthy memories. He couldn't believe his shitty luck. Sometimes, he wondered if meeting her was payback for all the times others had found themselves in undesirable dating situations because of his app.

He yanked away from her a fraction of a moment before her scarlet-painted lips landed on his. "I didn't realize you were still in the area," he said to her, his jaw hard.

"I'm dating a Coastie now." Her smile faded a bit as she leaned in closer, providing him with an uninhibited view of her perky breasts spilling from the dress's plunging neckline. She'd initially caught his eye on his app because of them. Then Christina had revealed she was borderline certifiable and he found everything about her repulsive. "But it's nothing serious." She scratched a blood-red fingernail over the top button on his shirt. "We're free to do whatever we want with other people."

Brock gathered her wandering hand from his chest and inwardly groaned. He hoped this Coastie knew he'd stumbled into a cobra's nest by dating her. "You need to move on, Christina. Nothing's going to happen between us ever again. You made sure of that when you started that lawsuit."

"I had no other choice after what you did to me." Her petite features hardened. "I may never experience a healthy relationship again because of the emotional damage you inflicted. I had picked out a wedding dress, Brock."

A gruff laugh ripped from his throat. "There was no indication we were headed down that path, and you know it."

The door opened again and Knox emerged in a tight black button-down and black jeans. Brock grunted happily. He'd never been so relieved to see his oldest buddy.

"Christina!" he greeted her with mock enthusiasm. "I was hoping I'd never have to see you again!"

Her clear blue eyes rolled toward the dark sky. "The feeling's mutual, Deputy Doofus."

Any trace of humor evaporated from Knox's expression as he stood a little taller, taking on what

Brock fondly thought of as his official police mode. "I thought you agreed to stay away from my boy so he wouldn't have to file a restraining order against you."

"I came here with a date," she pouted before gesturing toward Brock. "How was I supposed to know he would be here?"

"Doesn't matter," Knox insisted with a firm head shake. "He's here now. That's your cue to leave."

"Don't bother trying to make her listen," Brock told him, glancing over his shoulder to peer through the open doorway. The sight of women in fashionable dresses and men in suits sipping champagne and plastering on artificial smiles made his skin crawl. He knew all too well those types of soirees were mere fodder for town gossip. "I changed my mind about being here anyway."

"Take me with you," Christina begged, gripping his forearm. "We can catch up over drinks."

"Give it a rest already!" Knox snarled while prying her fingers from Brock's arm. "Keep this up, and I'm hauling your crazy ass downtown for disorderly conduct!"

She cradled her hand as if he'd wounded it. "And I'll sue you for police brutality!"

"If you're smart, Christina, you'll stay the hell away from me," Brock warned. He raced down the stairway with Knox two steps behind. Their long strides matched step-for-step as they hustled toward Brock's silver Tesla. Christina continued yelling Brock's name every step of the way.

Knox let out a wheezing laugh as he approached the passenger's side of the car. "Changed your mind about that restraining order yet, buddy?"

Brock grunted in response to the question, thinking it was a wise idea. Then he frowned. "Where's your truck?"

"I caught a ride with that banker lady I met at your brewery a couple weeks back. I'm pretty sure she's intent on getting into the DA's pants by the end of the night, so I'm catching a ride with you."

"Did you see Andy in there?" Brock asked, lifting his chin at the house.

Knox's eyebrows shot upward. "You mean your hot new bartender? No, man. I don't think she'd be into the party scene."

Brock let out a short chuckle. "How would you know? You met her for all of a minute."

"I got some strange vibes off of her when she met like she's hiding something."

"You're just butt-hurt that she didn't react to your charm like most women," Brock assured him, ready to change the conversation. They opened the car's doors and slipped inside simultaneously.

"I don't know, man," Knox continued, eyeing him thoughtfully from the passenger seat. "Has she told you *anything* about herself, like maybe why she left Cave Junction and came here without having a job or housing lined up?"

"You're off duty, officer. Give it a rest." Brock engaged the motor and let out a breath edged with irritation. He eyed the house, wondering how long before he'd run into Christina again. "What is it with you and me and women? We're in our mid-thirties. Shouldn't we have them figured out by now? Is there some kind of handbook we're missing out on?"

"This comes from a guy who made his fortune from pairing couples."

"It obviously proves I understand the science of relationships, but I personally don't know jack-shit about women."

Smirking, Knox quirked a lone eyebrow. "Are you saying you still haven't made any progress with Andy?"

"I'm still trying to figure her out. She claims she isn't interested in starting a relationship, but the way she reacts to my subtle flirting is on a different level. I'm starting to think her past is so complicated that she's not interested in getting involved with anyone."

Knox patted Brock's shoulder. "You're probably better off not knowing the answer to that."

After stopping by a few happening bars down by the bay, Knox became interested in reconnecting with an old flame when Brock decided to call it a night. Brock walked alone to the brewery to check in on his employees and catch a sober ride home. He hoped he might even catch a glimpse of Andy. A few times, she had hung out at the bar on her nights off, conversing with staff while nursing a beer but otherwise keeping to herself.

He was so busy thinking of what to say to her that he nearly collided with her on the sidewalk behind the building.

"Imagine meeting you here," she said to him, grinning.

Confusion rippled through his thoughts as he briefly eyed her black sweatpants and black sweatshirt. She looked prepared for a break-in. "What are you doing out here in the dark?"

"Just getting a little fresh air."

"It's *dark,*" he repeated.

"And you're *drunk,*" she fired back. Her lips twisted with a smirk. "You seem to have a problem staying away from this place, even when intoxicated. Maybe we should switch housing since you practically live here anyway."

"Or you could just stay with me," he suggested, wiggling his eyebrows. "You would still have your own space. We probably wouldn't run into each other for days on end."

"You're funny when you're drunk."

"I'm not drunk. And I'm being serious."

"You're asking me to move in with you?" Laughing brightly, she waved a hand through the air. "If you're not drunk, you have to be high. I'm still the same girl who stole your credit card."

"Desperate situations call for desperate measures. You were on the run and had no other choice."

"I had another choice," she said, her voice all at once faint. "I just wasn't brave enough to choose it."

He tilted his head at the brewery. "Come join me for a drink inside…on the house."

"How are you getting home?"

"I'm gonna call for a ride."

"It's after midnight on a Monday night, Brock. They stopped offering services hours ago."

"Then I'll walk."

"I guess I can give you a ride," she said reluctantly. "Where's your car?"

"Down by the bay."

She dropped her head back and forced out a harsh sigh. "Then I suppose you can crash on the couch, considering it's *your* apartment, but only if you promise to stay on the couch and keep things strictly platonic."

"I can do platonic," he promised.

Until he followed her up the ancient, steep stairway to the apartment, he hadn't realized she was right. He was definitely drunk. He was also grateful she'd led the way so she wouldn't witness him bracing a hand against the brick wall the entire way to stop himself from swaying.

Once she unlocked the door and stepped inside, he was practically on her heels. She turned to say something and gasped, surprised to find him so nearby.

Her bright green eyes locked with his, filling his chest with a warm, silky heat. He could sense she was equally turned on when her breaths became labored, and her chest rose a little higher each time. They were close enough that he could've leaned forward a few inches, and their mouths would connect.

"Platonic, remember?" she whispered, her eyes regretfully trailing to his lips.

"Come walk the Riverwalk with me on Friday," he told her.

"Let me think about it," she answered with a sly look as she stepped back. "I'm not convinced it's a good idea for us to spend time alone." She started for the stairway leading up to the loft, pausing to throw him a reluctant smile. "Good night, Brock."

Later, when he heard her soft breaths filling the small apartment, he was convinced he'd never be able to sleep. She was so temptingly close, yet still so far away.

CHAPTER 7

Andy

"WHY DID *that man call you a pirate?"*

Her question was met with a deep, joyful chuckle. "Because I hunt for treasure, darlin'."

"Are you a REAL pirate?"

The man cupped her chin and grinned. "You bet your sweet little buns I am."

Andy woke with a start and stared at the apartment ceiling, feeling comfort when hearing Brock's steady breaths filling the darkness. The same man who had told her to be a good girl had started appearing in nearly every single one of her dreams. The dreams were always different. His features weren't exactly clear, yet something about his voice felt so familiar. Who was he?

Early Thursday afternoon, before her evening shift began, Andy visited Skye's boutique, intending to find something halfway flirty to wear in case she decided to take Brock up on his offer to explore the Riverwalk Trail together. Skye's Unlimited was bright and airy, painted all white, and decorated with natural wood furnishings. There was always something cheery and uplifting playing from the speakers, and a wonderfully floral scent clung to every square inch. At first, Andy enjoyed visiting Skye's shop merely for its spa-like atmosphere. Then she'd grown fond of the style of clothing Skye offered, and had vowed to buy an item from her once every week. She didn't necessarily care if others were beginning to notice her wardrobe was minuscule...it simply made her feel more human.

That afternoon, half a dozen female customers browsed the generous clothing racks as Andy casually shopped alongside them. Behind the podium used as a checkout counter, Skye wore a black dress with a colorful kimono over the top, brown hair curled loosely around her shoulders. With a cordless phone pressed to her ear, she spotted Andy and gave a friendly wave before holding up a finger to indicate she'd be a minute. Andy waved back and nodded before plucking several flowing blouses and sweaters off of a sale rack. Although she sensed she'd never been much of a girly girl, she came across a navy body-con dress that felt luxurious against her fingertips and decided to try it on—if only for fun.

She helped herself to one of the curtain-clad dressing spaces and changed into her selected items. Several of them nailed the look she was going for, but she narrowed it down to a simple white sweater with small gold buttons on the sides. She'd received her first regular paycheck several days before and needed to save up as much as she could for whatever crisis may come next. When she finally got to the dress, she marveled at how it fit her like a glove. Although she had laughed to herself when she recalled Meghan telling her she could be an influencer, she suddenly wasn't so sure the girl had been wrong. She looked *amazing*.

"Hey, Andy!" Skye called out from the other side of the white suede curtain. "Finding anything you like?"

"As a matter of fact, I found something I intend to buy." Andy spun around to admire her shapely backside in the mirror. "Now I'm just trying on something for fun."

"Ooo. Can I see?"

Andy nibbled on her bottom lip as she glanced at

the attached price tag. She couldn't afford the dress and worried she'd offend Skye if she left it behind. "Sure," she answered in a flat tone.

The curtain was jerked aside and Skye let out a squeal that caught the attention of every last patron. "Andy, you look absolutely stunning! Like...*wow*, girlfriend!"

Two women peering over her shoulder nodded enthusiastically.

"Thanks." Andy's cheeks burned hot as she tugged the curtain back into place. She couldn't afford that kind of attention if she wanted to stay safely hidden. Before she could reach for the gold zipper that started at the base of the V hem between her shoulder blades and continued all the way down to the bottom hem, Skye stepped into the dressing room beside her.

"Sorry, I wasn't trying to embarrass you." She shook her head as her warm brown gaze swept over the dress again. "It's just...*wow.* If my brother saw you in that—"

"He's my boss," Andy reminded her sharply.

"So what? It's not like he's the President and you're his intern."

Andy sighed. Skye had a point. Too bad it wasn't the only reason holding her back. "My history is too complicated. I don't want to drag him into it."

"We all have complicated histories, sister." Folding her arms beneath her chest, Skye quirked her eyebrows. "They don't necessarily define who we are."

Andy glanced at her reflection in the mirror, unconvinced that was the case. Was she a thief? A murderer? Certainly those crimes would define her character if they were proven to be true.

"Hell," Skye continued with a huff, "if you knew what I was like ten years ago, we probably wouldn't be having this conversation. My own parents cut me out of their lives. I'm just fortunate I have a brother who loved me enough to put up with my crap and help me straighten things out. Without him, I'd probably be dead. Instead, he funded this place and helped me start a new life...one that I can finally be proud of. And the real kicker is he won't let me pay him back for any of it. Whenever I've tried, he's donated the money to the women's shelter downtown. Now, I donate directly to the shelter."

Andy's eyes filled with empathetic tears. She had already sensed the siblings were close long before she'd learned of Brock's generosity toward his sister. A part of her wished Skye hadn't told her the details. Andy had a difficult enough time resisting Brock's charisma already. When she'd offered for him to spend the night on the apartment couch, she hadn't been convinced she could stop herself from inviting him to join her in the loft bed.

Andy grabbed the sweater she intended to purchase and handed it to Skye. "I'm going to get this and probably a set of earrings too." The other night, she had noticed that her ears were pierced and decided she should start wearing earrings to work like the other girls, if only to fit in.

The golden flecks in Skye's dark eyes seemed to dance when they flickered back to the dress. "Sure you don't want that too? Forget what I said about my brother. You don't need it for some guy, anyway. That looks as if it was made specifically for you. If I had a body like that, I'd want to show it off as much as possible. I'll give it to you for half price just because I think you should have it."

"That's extremely sweet of you, but I don't have any reason to wear a dress," Andy insisted, waving her away. She had already taken advantage of the siblings' generosity too many times. She wasn't sure she deserved it.

"I think that was my new favorite movie," she declared with a happy little skip.

"Oh yeah?" the man asked, swinging their joined hands. "What was your favorite part?"

"They were hunting for treasure right here in Oregon!"

The man chuckled in a deep, rolling sound. "That's because sometimes art imitates life, baby girl. And sometimes there are truths to fiction."

An urgent knock on the apartment door roused Andy from her latest dream involving the same man. Her nocturnal memories were becoming more frequent. What was her brain trying to tell her?

With the pistol stuffed inside the back of the pajama pants from Skye's boutique, she headed down to the door and glanced out the peephole. Meghan stood rigid outside her door, mascara streaked down her cheeks, eyes wild with raw fear. Her normally envious hair hung in clumps around her face like she'd recently gone for a swim and let it air dry. She'd been working earlier and still wore a T-shirt with the brewery's logo beneath a white zip-up hoodie. The T-shirt's neckline was torn.

Andy quickly unlocked the door and caught the sobbing girl in her arms when she lurched forward. "Meghan? What's wrong?"

"I—I didn't know w-where e-else to go!" She

cried even harder, her entire body violently trembling.

"Come on," Andy prodded, leading her to the couch. "Deep breaths, Meghan. You're safe now." She moved a section of the girl's blond hair over her shoulder, finding her coworker's eye swollen and red. First shock, then white-hot rage blossomed deep inside Andy's chest. "Who hurt you?"

"I c-an't tell you!" she stuttered, snot dripping from her nose. "He'd k-kill me!"

"Was it Jake?" Andy seethed through gritted teeth. Although Meghan's boyfriend was considered the town's golden boy, Andy knew boys like him could put on a good show for adults, even though she didn't know how she acquired that knowledge.

Hunched over, Meghan repeatedly shook her head in reply.

"Come on, Meghan. Either you tell me, or I have to call the cops."

The young girl's entire body convulsed. "You can't call the cops! Please don't!"

Anger heated Andy's veins. "Then tell me who did this to you."

"It's my fault," Meghan whispered, cupping her face with her hands. "I stood up to him after I broke curfew."

"Your *father* did this?"

"You can't tell anyone." Meghan swiped an arm across her eyes, leaving a trail of black mascara over her white sweatshirt sleeve. She inhaled a slow breath, all at once appearing angry. "The cops wouldn't do anything to him anyway. He's always reminding me and my sisters that he's invincible."

We'll see about that, Andy thought bitterly as she rubbed circles into the girl's bony back. She felt immense guilt for telling Meghan to stand up to men. Had she known Meghan's father was being abusive, the conversation would've gone in an entirely different direction.

She somehow had to make it right.

She patted the throw pillow at the end of the couch. "Why don't you lay down here for a while and give him some time to cool down?"

Exhausted settled over Meghan's features as she nodded. "O-okay," she hiccuped.

Andy carefully draped the blanket over the teenager and continued rubbing her back until she drifted asleep. Meghan didn't stir as Andy slipped out of the apartment.

Stars winked high above the sleepy town as Andy crept onto the immaculate lawn of the stately mansion. When Andy spotted Meghan's sporty sedan parked in the driveway, the writing on her rear window from homecoming week was still faintly visible, and she knew she was in the right place. She tugged the hood of her sweatshirt down around her face and made a beeline for the second car parked in the driveway—a shiny new, cherry-red sports car with custom plates that read: DSTATTY.

Gripping the cast iron skillet from the apartment with both hands, she swung down on the center of the windshield, feeling a thrill of satisfaction with the sight of the spiderwebbed hole. A high alarm pierced the air, and the car's headlights flashed as she swung the skillet again, leaving a massive dent in the spotless hood.

"What in the hell are you doing?" a gruff voice demanded. "Step away from the car! I'm calling the police!"

Andy spun around to face a fit, middle-aged man standing on the wide steps leading up to the mansion's front door. With a generous headful of blond hair and sharp features, he was good-looking like his daughter but appeared notably vulnerable in a pair of navy pajamas, a cell phone gripped in one hand.

"Go ahead and call them," she challenged. "Call

them and explain how you're a piece of shit who abuses his children."

She felt a jolt of satisfaction when his mask of anger slipped for a moment. He had all but admitted it was true. "Whoever the hell you are, you don't know a damn thing about me and my family!" he finally roared. "Get off my property!"

The skillet clattered onto the driveway as Andy reached for the pistol inside her waistband. She aimed the weapon at his head, hands steady as her pointed finger hovered over the trigger. A soothing calm spread over her nerves like she'd trained for that moment.

Meghan's father dropped his cell phone onto the concrete step and slowly raised the palms of his hands. "Now hold on—"

"Consider this a courtesy call, District Attorney. Lay a hand on one of your daughters again, and I will end you. Do you understand?"

His face glowered a dark shade of red beneath the porch light. "I don't know who you think you are, but that's a terroristic threat, you crazy b—"

"That's no *threat,*" she corrected, lowering the gun. "It's a promise. One I intend to keep."

CHAPTER 8

Brock

BROCK WAS on his second cup of coffee when Knox shuffled in through his back door in full uniform, eyes shadowed, shoulders slumped. Seeing his old buddy in that condition reminded Brock of Friday nights in high school when they'd party all night and check in for their shifts at the same seafood restaurant late the next morning, pumped full of energy drinks.

"Smells good." Knox removed his Astoria PD ball cap and sighed deeply while scratching his head. "Got any left?"

"Help yourself." Brock motioned to the gourmet coffee pot from his perch at the sleek kitchen island. "Isn't it a little early for you to be on duty, Officer?"

"I'm just coming off a shift," his buddy grumbled, pouring the black liquid into a mug featuring Brock's alma matter's mascot of an angry red bird. "Some chick vandalized the DA's new Ferrari with an iron skillet in the middle of the night. He claims he doesn't know anyone with a grudge against him, but the chief thinks it's one of his many mistresses, disgruntled because he won't leave his wife." With a smirk, Knox slipped a thumb inside his duty belt and raised his mug. "Between you and me, I'm glad to see the self-righteous prick humbled for a change."

"His middle daughter works for me," Brock reminded him. "Meghan's a good kid. I hope you find this woman before she takes her anger out on his family."

Knox nodded thoughtfully while slurping his coffee. "The funny thing is, the suspect was caught on the DA's security camera. The image was blurred, and her face was shadowed from a hoodie, but we were able to make out the words printed on her sweatshirt. Wanna know what it said?" His eyes remained steady on Brock's when he continued. "Cave Junction."

The heat drained from Brock's face. *Like Andy's sweatshirt*. "Interesting."

"Yeah…*real* interesting," Knox agreed with a tilt of his head. "Know anyone with a sweatshirt like that?"

Looking away, Brock shrugged. "It's a popular

attraction. I'm sure dozens of residents around here have one. Hell, don't *you* have one?"

"Mhmm. Seems like you're not being straightforward with me, brother."

Brock shot him an irritated scowl. "Just because Andy has a sweatshirt like that doesn't mean she's your suspect."

Knox arched one eyebrow. "You sure about that? How well do you actually know her?"

"I'd bet serious money she isn't capable of that type of violence. Besides, she wouldn't have any reason to go after the DA. She keeps to herself… hardly ever leaves the apartment."

"Maybe she's been sleeping with him."

"She's definitely not!" Brock snarled.

"How would you know?"

"I just do."

A strange look briefly crossed Knox's eyes. "Are *you* sleeping with her?"

"No." Brock shot to his feet and began pacing the hickory floor. "If you knew her like I do, you'd know she isn't good for something like this."

"Oh yeah? Then what's her deal? Why is she here?"

With a flare of anger, Brock blurted, "She's running from an abusive ex, alright? I didn't tell you before because sharing her business is not my place.

But she's a victim, Knox. If she had the kind of aggression you're suggesting, I'm sure she would've stayed in Cave Junction and stood up to the asshole. Instead, she fled here. She's too afraid to leave the apartment on her own."

"*That's* her story?" With a curt laugh, Knox lowered the coffee mug. "And you believe her?"

"Why shouldn't I?"

"The old 'abusive ex' story seems a bit improbable with someone like her." Grunting, Knox dumped the remainder of his coffee into the stainless steel sink and set the empty cup on the granite counter top. "I'm gonna try to catch a few hours of sleep before heading back to the station." He stepped toward the door and paused with his back to Brock. "Call if you decide you know something that might be relevant to this case."

Unease swirled through Brock's gut as his buddy shut the door behind him. He'd thought it strange when Andy had been dressed in black from head to toe the other night. Maybe there was far more to the mysterious blonde-turned-burnette than he knew.

Brock's suspicions that Andy was the one who had vandalized the DA's car grew when she showed up in uniform to cover Meghan's shift rather than ready for the walk he'd suggested. He watched her work with a new perspective, wondering just how much she was hiding. She never spoke about herself, failing to provide a hint of anything from her favorite color to where she'd lived as a child.

Once he'd started seeing glimpses of her true personality a few weeks earlier, he didn't want her leaving Astoria any time soon. He'd begun to fear she'd be out of his life as quickly as she'd entered.

Now, he wasn't exactly sure what he wanted from her.

A stupid sweatshirt certainly didn't make her guilty like Knox had suggested. There were over 10,000 residents in Astoria. There had to be other suspects in the area with actual motives.

Concerned Meghan's absence had something to do with the attack on her father, Brock approached Andy as she was giving Greg, his only college employee, a high-five. "Where's Meghan?" he asked.

"She wasn't feeling well," Andy explained with a half-hearted shrug.

"She told you that?" Brock pressed, frowning. "Did she mention the incident at her house last night?"

"You mean the crazy lady that effed-up her old man's sweet ride?" Greg asked, grinning. "I bet that dude was *pissed*. He cares more about his toys than his family."

Brock merely shook his head. What they said was true—small town gossip spread faster than wildfire.

When a group of customers approached the register, Greg excused himself to wait on them. Brock tugged Andy in the opposite direction. "Where were you last night?" he asked, carefully scrutinizing her reaction.

"Home," she answered. Her vivid green gaze narrowed. "Why?"

"Knox told me the woman that vandalized the DA's car was wearing a Cave Junction sweatshirt."

Unflinching, she let out a snorting laugh. "Are you insinuating I did it because of a generic sweatshirt I happen to own? I don't even know the guy." She leaned in a little closer and lowered her voice. "You have every right to question my integrity after I stole from you, but I'm not some thug, alright? I only took your credit card because I was scared for my life."

"Are you being straight with me?"

Her expression became cautious, then uneasy. "What would you do if I told you it *was* me? What if I told you I did it for a damn good reason? Would you turn me into your buddy, Knox?"

Unable to tell if she was being facetious, he

searched her bright-eyed gaze for the truth. "I'd believe you and help you however I can."

A dusty shade of pink rose in her pretty cheeks. *Was she regretting her recent nocturnal activities?* he wondered. "You'd believe me? Just like that?"

"Just like that," he confirmed. "I'd like to believe you're a good person with good intentions."

Her stunned expression remained glued to his face as Greg interrupted them. "Hey, do we offer gift cards?"

"In increments of twenty-five dollars," Andy answered without breaking Brock's quizzical stare. "They're on the first shelf underneath the register."

"Thanks?" Greg responded with a quick chuckle before returning to the register.

"Why would you think I'm a good person?" she asked Brock.

"I have a sense for these things."

"You can't possibly know what kind of person I am." She finally broke his stare and muttered, "I don't even know what kind of person I am."

What was that supposed to mean? he wondered. "Have dinner with me tonight."

Her eyebrows, a shade of dirty blond that hinted at her natural hair color, shot upward. "Is that an order from my boss?"

"It's a request from a friend. Can we forget for one night that I'm your boss?"

"Why, because you want to pursue your attraction toward me?"

He chuckled. "Has anyone told you that you're extremely straightforward?"

"I like you, Brock, but getting involved with me isn't a good idea. For either one of us."

"Because you're afraid of what your ex might do if he finds out you're with another man?"

She huffed out an exasperated breath. "Because I'm afraid of what *I* might do. This isn't a good time for me to get involved with someone. I have a lot going on that you know nothing about."

"So fill me in." He turned on the charming smile that normally made women putty in his hands but didn't seem to have any effect on Andy. "As far as I can tell, you haven't spent time with anyone outside of work except my sister. Let me take you to my favorite steak and seafood place on the waterfront. I'll drive you around after, show you the sites. You'll be safe with me, Andy. I promise."

She nibbled her lip, unintentionally tempting him to do the same. He sensed his attraction was reciprocated, but she held back because she was his employee. *Or maybe it was because the asshole she'd been with ruined her for the kind of decent man she deserves,* he thought with a silent grunt.

"I'm not sure about the steakhouse," she decided. "The nicest thing I own is a white sweater from your sister's shop...and these jeans."

Brock bit back a grin. Skye mentioned that Andy had fallen in love with a dress from her boutique but claimed she had nowhere to wear it. After Andy's shift started that morning, he'd given his sister an extra set of keys to the apartment and asked her to drop off the dress and whatever accessories Andy would need for a night on the town. Skye had squealed so loudly that he was sure she'd busted his ear drums.

"Whatever you decide to wear will be perfectly fine with me," he told Andy, shifting away so she wouldn't see just how much the idea of her in a fitting dress turned him on. Even if she showed up in the dusty zip-up shirt she'd been wearing when she'd stolen his card, he doubted he'd be able to contain his need to kiss her for much longer. "I'll come by at seven to pick you up," he called over his shoulder.

If she was, in fact, responsible for the destruction of the district attorney's car, he would bet his entire fortune she legitimately had a good reason for doing so like she claimed. For whatever reason, he liked her. A lot. She was attractive and smart and didn't seem interested in entertaining anyone's bullshit, including his.

On his way back to his office, he caught the glint of metal from the corner of his eye. Turning to face the street through the tall windows, he discovered Knox parked across the street in his police cruiser. Watching intently.

Brock lifted his hand in greeting. Knox only stared back at him.

CHAPTER 9

Andy

WHEN ANDY RETURNED to the apartment to change for her date with Brock, she was torn from her comfortable bubble and reminded of her looming fate. The piece of string she stretched out at the base of the door every morning was missing. Her blood ran ice cold through her veins, sending a chill down her spine. What if someone who'd known what happened in Cave Junction had somehow located her and had come for the diamond? Her heart all but exploded in her chest when she reached for the doorknob. At least it was still locked.

With a trembling hand, she slipped her key into the lock. Before pushing on the door, she positioned the key between the pointer and middle finger on her right hand, prepared to strike. She reached for the light switch, breath held as the room was flooded with an artificial glow. She continued holding her breath while straining to listen for the slightest noise to indicate she wasn't alone. The apartment remained blissfully silent.

Once she spotted the familiar reusable bag on the coffee table featuring the logo for Skye's Unlimited, she finally let out a trembling breath. Still, she crept up to the bed to retrieve the pistol and headed into the bathroom to assure herself the blue diamond was still in the same spot where she'd left it her first night there. It seemed Skye was behind the "break-in," although she sensed Brock had a hand in it too.

She was prepared to wear the Cave Junction sweatshirt and her old jeans to make a point to Brock and his pushy sister until she peered inside the bag to find the dress she'd tried on with a pair of gold heels and coordinating jewelry. The dress was truly made with the softest material she'd ever felt, and she had to admit she had looked fabulous when she tried it on.

Nevertheless, she remained angry at the siblings for coming uninvited into what was supposed to be her safe space. As she wiggled out of her jeans, she realized there was a much more efficient way to get her point across to Brock.

Andy wasn't sure if she'd ever curled her hair or applied makeup before until she began beautifying with the supplies Skye had brought over the first night. She surprised herself by completely transforming her looks. "Would've been good to know you possessed this skill sooner," she scolded her reflection. By the time she was finished, a small part of her wondered if she'd been a makeup artist, a spy, or a runway model.

When she opened the door for Brock, his jaw slacked as if its hinges had simply given out. The bouquet of daisies he held sagged in his grip.

"Something wrong?" she purred, shifting her hips several times so the soft material would slink against her thighs.

"You're…holy shit."

The sentiment warmed her all over. It felt good to be admired that way. If she had been in a more ideal position, one that didn't involve her being on the run from something unknown, she would've dragged him close and ravaged his pillowy lips. Instead, she fluttered her eyelashes coated in several layers of mascara. "You like it?"

His tongue appeared to wet his lips. "Like isn't a strong enough word."

With a dramatic sigh, she turned to face the apartment's interior. "You know, I'm suddenly not feeling the best. I think I'll stay here and watch a little TV." She turned back to him. "Raincheck?"

"You can't be serious," he grumbled under his breath before his eyes narrowed on her tight lips. "Are you mad at me for some reason?"

"You're more perceptive than I thought." With a humorless laugh, she crossed her arms and leaned against the doorframe. "How did your sister get inside this apartment?"

"I gave her a key." He shook his head. "That's why you're mad?"

"Depends. Are you the only one with an extra key, or can I expect all of Astoria to pay me an unannounced visit at some point?"

He briefly scrubbed his handsome face with both hands. "I'm sorry. I should've mentioned it."

"You should've told her she could wait to stop by when I was home."

"You're right. I screwed up. I've become so comfortable around you that I sometimes forget the reason you came to Astoria."

Laughter died in her throat. If he knew the real reason she was in Astoria, she wished he'd share.

He ducked his chin and gave her a guilt-ridden look. "I promise I won't let anyone use the key again unless there's some kind of emergency. Will you forgive me?"

Despite the amused smile against her lips, she wasn't convinced she should let him off so quickly. Still, he was so damn irresistible in a gray sports jacket and white button-down with jeans that it was downright impossible to stay mad.

Despite the cluster of people waiting to be seated at the charming little restaurant several blocks down from the brewery, Brock convinced the redheaded hostess to seat them immediately. The way the pretty hostess blushed and lowered her chin bashfully before leaving them alone, Andy suspected she was among the women Brock had "pampered" in the past. With a sudden paranoia, Andy studied the other patrons in the upscale restaurant featuring black leather booths and low-hung crystal chandeliers. She felt dangerously exposed away from the safety of the brewery and the apartment. Maybe she was becoming too comfortable in Astoria. She had paid her debt to Brock and had slipped a wad of cash into Skye's purse the previous afternoon when she hadn't been looking. Maybe it was time to move on.

"Everything okay?" Brock asked.

Spine straight, Andy grinned at him over the tapered candles in the center of the little round table covered in a black tablecloth. "Why do I feel as if I'm dining with Astoria's most eligible bachelor?"

"I don't have time to date," he grumbled, snagging one of the menus the redhead had left behind. His eyes darted over the items as if only pretending to read the contents he probably had memorized. By the delightful aroma swirling through the air, she guessed everything tasted amazing anyway.

Andy took the other menu and idly ran her fingers along the leather cover. As always, she saw right through his lies. He must've been a terrible poker player. She also sensed he wasn't kidding when he claimed he would help her if she had truly been responsible for punishing Meghan's father. She debated on whether or not to tell him everything. Would he repeat her story to Knox?

"How bad were things with this boyfriend?" Brock suddenly blurted, glancing up at her with worry etched into his expression.

"He's my ex," she decided. "We hadn't been together in a really long time."

His shoulders tensed. "How bad did he hurt you?"

"I'm not really sure." As a rush of warmth spread through her, she ran her fingertips over where the knot had been on the back of her head. She enjoyed how Brock made her feel and didn't want to have to feed him fabricated bits of the truth any longer. But she feared he wouldn't want anything to do with her if he knew the truth. "I...uh...must've blacked out. When I woke, he was gone, and there was a massive gash in the back of my head."

Fire shone through his gaze. "Jesus, Andy! Did you have it checked out?"

"I didn't think it was safe. I had to leave before he found me again and finished the job."

Brock reached out to take one of her hands in his. "Did he hurt you anywhere else?"

She lightly squeezed his warm hand, trying not to cry. Too much time had passed since she woke in the forest, and she was becoming increasingly lonely. His touch awakened her need for a deeper connection and reminded her of all the things she didn't deserve. Including him. "I don't think so."

He leaned over the table, voice lowered. "I'm taking you to see my personal physician in the morning. He's retired, and—"

"I don't need to see anyone," she told him with a firm shake of her head. "I'm fine, Brock. It's healed by now, and the headaches have gone away."

As his warm gaze held hers, his thumb swept back and forth over the back of her hand. "He would be discreet. He's been through this kind of thing before. He can be trusted."

"Can we talk about something else?" She pulled her hand away from his and threw him a teasing smile. "Tell me more about this dating app. Why do you and your best friend remain single if it's so successful?"

For a moment, he worked his jaw while looking back at her. "Will you please at least talk to someone else about what happened? Skye went through something similar—the prick was arrested but the prosecutor was unwilling to press charges because he was a city councilman. No one wanted to make waves."

Andy felt a blinding urge to slink beneath the table. It was no wonder the brother and sister duo had been so kind to her. But Andy was a fraud and didn't deserve their empathy. She stood, feeling trapped by her endless lies with no clear way to fix them. "I'm sorry, but I've lost my appetite." She turned away before he could talk her out of leaving.

His leather loafers clicked on the hardwood behind her as she raced outside. "Andy, wait!" As she rushed past the group waiting to enter the restaurant and gulped in the salty air, his fingers gently brushed over her forearm. "I'm sorry I pushed you on the subject. It's just...I don't want you to feel like you're all alone in this. I want to help you."

Tears burned behind her eyelids as she spun

around to face him. "It's more complicated than you think. I don't deserve your help."

Something tightened in her chest when he gently gripped her arms and threw her a tender look. "So tell me about it."

"I can't," she whispered against the knot in her throat.

"Why not?"

The truth bubbled up inside her chest. *Because I don't know who I am.* She'd give anything to have an ally, and she sensed she could trust Brock. But what would that trust cost him? If she killed the man in the forest, Brock could either be an accessory to her crime, or he could get caught in the middle if someone came after her for revenge.

"I'm sorry about dinner." She rose on her tiptoes and brushed her lips over his warm, clean-shaven cheek. "Thank you for everything."

When she backed away, he snagged her elbow. "Please don't go."

As she struggled with what to say, he leaned in and feathered his lips over hers. Her breath caught. It was a test of a kiss, a question if she wanted more. Her eyes found his as he cupped her face and leaned in to do it again. *This is a bad idea, she warned herself,* refusing to get swept into the second kiss. But his powerful lips and determined tongue worked together to put a spell on her that she was too weak to break. Soon, she was gripping his thick hair in her fists, answering every sweep of his tongue and every press of his lips. She could continue to deny how badly she wanted him, or she could allow herself to enjoy what he wanted to give her in whatever amount of time she stuck around. The concept of a meaningless fling wasn't too appealing but she felt wanted by him—a sensation she hadn't experienced since the moment she'd opened her eyes to that forest.

She was all alone with no one to turn to, no one to give their advice on what she should do next. If she ran away from Astoria, there wouldn't be anyone else who would miss her. No one would come looking. No one cared except Brock and his sister.

Yet she could not shake the feeling that she was doing something seriously wrong. Just because she hadn't been wearing a wedding ring when she lost her memory didn't mean she wasn't married or seriously committed to someone otherwise. And someone was bound to come looking for her and the diamond at some point. She couldn't drag Brock into her mess without fearing she'd put him in imminent danger, too.

"I can't," she panted, nudging him backward. "I'm sorry, Brock."

His lips, still red and raw from their kiss, formed a scowl. "Are you pushing me away because of your ex?" He brushed a section of her wavy hair over her bare shoulder, sensually dragging his fingertip across her skin. "He can't hurt you anymore, Andy. I won't let him."

The tears thickening her throat wouldn't allow her to say anything in return.

She turned away from him, intending to run away as fast as her heels would allow until she felt a slow, uneasy prickling sensation travel along her spine.

She sensed they were being watched by someone cloaked in the darkness.

CHAPTER 10

Brock

THE FOLLOWING MORNING, Brock heaved a sigh of relief when Andy marched into the brewery ten minutes before her scheduled shift. Although she was wearing jeans and a sweatshirt from his sister's boutique instead of her usual uniform, he was at least grateful she hadn't skipped town. There was no use pretending the kiss hadn't erased all his doubts or that he didn't want more. He'd driven all over looking for her after she'd run from the restaurant, and then he spent half the night contemplating ways he could convince her to stay. He was willing to do whatever it took—even if he had to back off and give her whatever space she needed.

"Good morning," he greeted her as she neared. "After what you said last night, I was afraid you'd—"

Her beautiful face hardened with ferocity as she stepped up close to him. "I thought you were a good man, but I guess I was wrong. I finally understand why someone like you is single." The tone of her voice deepened. "If you think you can intimidate me for rejecting you—"

"Hold on." He held a hand up between them, shaking his head. "Exactly how did I intimidate you?"

She barred her teeth. "Don't play dumb."

"Andy, I swear I have no idea what you're talking about."

Throat bobbing with a hard swallow, her green eyes widened. "You didn't pay a visit to the apartment sometime in the night while I was out for a run?"

"Why would I—" When her face paled, Brock wrapped his arm around her shoulders and led her to the nearest table. "Take a minute to catch your breath."

As she lowered to the chair, he noticed a slight bulge tucked into the back of her jeans. *Was she carrying a gun?* His mind began to race. Just how dangerous was this ex of hers?

He squatted on the floor at her side, taking her closest hand inside both of his. "What's going on, Andy?"

Her eyes darted around the brewery. "The apartment door was wide open when I returned from my run. The lock had been broken on the outside."

"You really think I would've vandalized my own property just to get your attention?" he scolded. "That's not my style." He released her hand and stood, running a shaking hand through his hair. Had her ex found her? Could it be Christina, feeling a renewed need to harass him after he blew her off the other night? He pulled his cell phone from his pocket. Although he didn't want to give Knox another reason to suspect something was up with Andy, he was more worried for her safety. "I'm calling Knox."

"No!" She shot to her feet, eyeing the door as if ready to flee. "No cops!"

"What if your ex is in town? Andy, it might not be safe for you to go back."

"You're right." Scrubbing her hands over her face, she released a heavy sigh. "I have to leave."

Brock narrowly resisted the urge to physically restrain her so she couldn't leave. "Then what? Are you going to run for the rest of your life? At least while you're here, you have me…and Skye."

Her hands lifted at her sides. "I can't stay here forever!"

"Why not?"

She turned away, gripping her hair in her fists, and let out an exasperated sound. Brock could sense the fear and frustration running through her veins, even if he didn't completely understand the reasoning since she refused to share anything personal.

He nudged her gently. "Come on. We're going for a ride."

Andy remained silent on the forty-five-minute drive to Cannon Beach, her gaze seemingly glued to the window at her side. But after Brock parked and led her toward the Haystack Rock, her face lit up like that of a little kid on Christmas morning.

"I've been here before," she announced, quickening her pace once their feet hit the sand. "I know this place!"

"Yeah?" Brock couldn't help but notice it sounded like she was having a conversation with herself. "It's a hotspot for tourists. Did you visit with your family?"

"I don't remember," she answered in a disappointed tone.

He stood still as he breathed in the salty air, wishing she'd divulge more. She claimed she didn't have anyone. Did it mean her parents were dead, or did they simply not get along? "Where'd you grow up?"

She all at once looked dazed as she continued walking without him. When he heard her mumble something, he quickly caught up with her again. "What's that?"

"I've been seeing this exact spot in my dreams," she whispered, eyes unwavering on the rock formation. "I've been here...with him."

"Your ex?"

"No." She turned to him with a dazed look. "Someone else. I think maybe my father."

"You told me you don't have any family to turn to."

Her gaze drifted away, skimming over the water as wind blew her hair around her face. She was breathtakingly beautiful at that moment despite the lost look in her eyes. "I haven't been completely honest with you."

A humorless laugh vibrated in his throat. "Am I supposed to act surprised?"

"I'm sorry. I can't tell you the whole story, but only because I think it's necessary to protect you from the truth."

"I don't need your protection, Andy." He smoothed a hand over her soft cheek, searching her bright green eyes for the explanation she refused to give. "I can handle whatever truths you throw at me."

"I did it," she blurted, pulling away from his touch. "I trashed that car with a cast iron skillet and threatened Meghan's dad. I had no other choice after she came to the apartment earlier that night, sporting a fresh shiner from him."

"That asshole hit her?" Brock bit out, his vision clouded by a rush of fury.

"Sounds like it's a regular occurrence with her and her sisters. She blamed herself for missing curfew and said the police wouldn't do anything if they knew."

Brock's teeth gnashed together. "You can bet your ass Knox would do something about it."

"Truthfully, it was my fault. I told her to stand up to men, but I meant the jerks at the brewery. I had no idea what was happening with her father, or I wouldn't have suggested it. I felt awful for putting the idea in her head. I had to do something to fix my mistake."

"So you bashed his car with a skillet?"

"He's lucky it wasn't his head. But I did more than that. I pulled a gun on him—one with a questionable history," she admitted, her eyes casting down to the sand surrounding their shoes. "I don't think he'll tell the police because he would have to make up a different threat, but if you tell Knox, I could go to prison…for a very long time."

"No one has to know about your involvement," Brock promised. "I can offer up an anonymous tip and leave it to him to investigate. Knox doesn't tolerate domestic abuse." He gripped her cold hands inside of his. "Andy, where'd you get the gun?"

"I-I don't know. I swear." She glanced at their hands locked together, visibly fighting the urge to pull away. "There are a lot of things I can't remember." Her eyes shone with tears when her gaze returned to his. "Starting with my name."

"You have amnesia?"

She gave a hesitant nod. "According to some articles I found online, it's likely dissociative amnesia. Normal amnesia from a head wound doesn't usually linger this long."

"Shit," he hissed. Although he'd suspected something unusual had happened to her, he didn't imagine it was anything to that extent. "When did it start?"

"Right before I stole your credit card. I woke in the forest outside of Cave Junction…with the gun…" She stopped to swallow with great difficulty. "And next to a dead body."

"A dead body?" he repeated with unease rushing down his back. "Did you recognize the person?"

She woefully shook her head. "I don't have any idea who I am, or what I might've done before I discovered him." Tears spilled down her cheeks when she added, "I'm so sorry I lied to you and your sister. You're both good people, and I took advantage."

Brock wasn't sure why he was so eager to take her for her word, except that he sensed she had a pure heart. He leaned down, pressing his forehead against hers. "I'd like you to stay at my house for a while. At least until we know who broke into the apartment. Maybe even until we uncover your identity."

"There's more to the story," she whispered. "I can't let you get involved in this."

"It's too late." He paused to press a soft, comforting kiss against her lips, salty from the air and her continuous tears. "I'm already involved, and I'm not walking away."

Leaning back on the apartment's couch, Brock studied the precious jewel clasped inside his fingers, marveling at its brilliance, clarity, and weight. He didn't have a ton of experience with diamonds. He'd been close to making the mistake of buying one his senior year in college for his girlfriend after he'd received his first royalty for the dating app. He was grateful he had decided against it once he discovered she'd been sleeping with his roommate.

"Hopefully, now you understand why I didn't openly ask anyone for help—at least not until I found someone I could trust," Andy explained from her perch on the cushion beside him. "I've decided to hold onto it until I can find its rightful owner."

He met her guilt-ridden gaze, dumbfounded. "Andy, this is easily more than ten carats. Maybe even thirteen. It must be worth a serious fortune."

She gave him an enthusiastic nod. "I was afraid to leave a digital trail, so the other day I did some research at the library." She paused to bite her lower lip. "A fifteen-carat blue diamond recently sold for nearly sixty million."

He whistled while shaking his head. "I think I liked it better when I thought you were running from a violent ex. That would've been far less complicated." *And less dangerous,* he decided. The rightful owner of something that valuable wouldn't give up their search for anything.

"Do you think I stole it?" she asked, her voice trembling.

"Watching you handle that handsy pervert at the

brewery and hearing how you threatened Meghan's dad for hurting her makes me believe you're no shrinking violet." He tossed the diamond back at her, grinning when she caught it with a surprised gasp. "But I don't believe you're a jewel thief. If you had come to me asking for my help in finding a seller for it, it'd be a different story. Your actions prove you're willing to fight for what's right."

Her eyes shone with unshed tears. "What about the dead man in the forest?"

Brock nudged one of her hands away from the diamond and laced their fingers together. "You're no killer either."

"I've been scouring the web since I moved here, searching for anything about a dead man or a wanted woman. You'd think someone would've come looking for me by now."

He shrugged. "Maybe whoever you recovered that diamond from is the thief in this scenario, and they're keeping what happened in that forest on the down low. It's possible they don't want any attention drawn to the situation until they've found you…and that diamond."

"What if they're the ones who broke into the apartment? What if they're here, in Astoria?"

His gut hardened. "I'll tell Knox we suspect your ex is in town and ask him to watch for any suspicious vehicles driving past my house. When he alluded to the fact that you could be involved with the DA's car, I had to throw him off your trail somehow, so I told him you were on the run from an abusive relationship. And you said you felt at ease with that gun, right?"

"I swear I've held it a thousand times before," she confirmed, releasing her tense shoulders with a deep sigh. "I truly appreciate that you believe in me, but what if you're wrong? What if I'm the bad guy in all of this?"

"You're not," he swore. "And I'm going to prove it."

"How?"

"I'm not sure, but I'll find a way." When Andy's expression filled with doubt, he squeezed her hand inside his. "You can question yourself all you want, but I've watched you from a distance for over two months. People can change, but their moral compass almost always stays the same. Everything you've done since I've met you proves you're a good person."

This time, she initiated the kiss.

CHAPTER 11

Andy

ONCE ANDY AGREED to stay overnight in Brock's modern home constructed of aged wood and black metal with enough floor-to-ceiling windows to provide a killer view of the bay, she insisted on sleeping in one of the three spare bedrooms. While she appreciated how easily he'd accepted the truth and had pledged his support, she was still afraid of what would happen if she fell any harder and cared any deeper for someone with such honorable intentions.

Although she didn't have a sense of what kind of economic status she came from, she had a feeling it was nowhere as elaborate as Brock's lifestyle. The mansion's furnishings were understated, but their quality wasn't anything one would find in a discount store. Quite frankly, it overwhelmed her and solidified the fact that she didn't belong with Brock. As she watched the sunset from the guest room, marveling at the pink and golden hues stretched behind the Astoria-Megler bridge, she realized she didn't even belong in Astoria.

She swore she'd just fallen asleep when she was jarred awake by the shrill wail of police sirens and shouting voices. Her sharp, panicked breaths pierced the darkness as she shot out of bed and began stuffing her belongings into the leather duffel bag Brock loaned her when she'd packed her meager belongings from the apartment. She'd been a fool to trust him with the truth. He'd charmed her with his good looks and had pretended to be supportive, only to trap her like a fly in a twisted web. He must've insisted on placing the blue diamond in his elaborate master bedroom safe only so he could turn it over to the police.

"Andy!" Brock hollered from the hallway, pounding on the locked bedroom door. "Andy, are you in there? Open up!"

Heart leaping into her throat, her eyes snapped over to the wall of windows flanking the end of the bedroom. She was only on the second floor, but the pitch of the house made the drop perilous. She could easily miss the patio on the recessed main floor and drop to her death on the rocks below.

"You have ten seconds to open this door before I break it down!" Brock warned, knocking more aggressively. "Knox caught my stalker outside, slashing my tires! I need to see for myself that she didn't get to you first! I need to see that you're okay!"

Slapping a hand over her feral heart, she released a stuttering breath. She'd been wrong about him and had completely misread the situation.

The second she opened the bedroom door, Brock swooped in to gather her inside his arms. "You scared the hell outta me!"

"That makes us even," she grumbled, allowing him to embrace her without reciprocating. Truthfully, she was afraid to move as only a thin piece of cotton covered her breasts, and she worried he'd notice her nipples had hardened. "What's this about a stalker?"

With a nervous chuckle, he released her. "You're not the only one with secrets. There was this woman from Sacramento—Christina—she went a little crazy after I told her it wouldn't work between us. She called me every hour on the hour for months, begging me to take her back. When that didn't work, she tried filing a bogus lawsuit for ten million, said I caused her irreversible emotional damage. I hadn't heard from her in several months until the other night at Meghan's house, but I suspect she's been following me this whole time. She must've finally lost her shit when she saw I had an overnight guest." His lips twisted with a deep scowl. "I have a strong feeling she's the one who broke into your apartment too."

Andy gestured to the bag she'd hastily packed. "Great, so I can go back there now?"

"Sorry to interrupt," Knox called out, stepping in behind Brock in a casual sweatsuit and sneakers, "but we should have everything we need from you to arrest Miss Psycho Pants outside. My partner's taking her down to the station for processing."

"Is that the official term for criminals?" Brock asked dryly.

"Don't bust my balls," his buddy groaned with a dramatic roll of his eyes. "We both know it's fitting after everything she's put you through." When he noticed Andy's skimpy pajamas, he snapped his head in the other direction. "Everything okay in here?"

"Everything's good," Brock assured him.

"Glad to hear it," he replied, clearing his throat. "It's probably a good idea for Andy to stay here until we're sure Christina was behind the attack on the apartment, too." He dared a glance back in her direction. "I don't know what *exactly* you're running from, Andy, but I know enough to suspect you're on the run from something bigger than you're telling us. I better not learn you had something to do with that body they found in the forest near Cave Junction."

Andy's heart stopped.

They'd found him. Had the man's identity been revealed? She didn't dare show any interest by asking. At least she'd become skilled enough at deception since she'd arrived in Astoria that she could stop herself from reacting in any way.

"Now you're accusing her of murder?" Brock snarled. "Thanks for your help, *Officer*, but I think it's time for you to head out."

Gripping the back of his buddy's neck, Knox stage-whispered, "You better hope she isn't more dangerous than the nut-job outside."

Neither Andy nor Brock moved until they heard the tall front door swoosh shut behind Knox. Then they raced together into the living room and he pressed a button on a remote that revealed a giant flatscreen TV behind an elaborate painting of a sail-boat in a raging sea.

"Try the local news first," she suggested, bouncing on her heels as he thumbed through the stations. She didn't have a sense of the time, but based on the amount of infomercials and reruns of old sitcoms, she assumed the evening news was finished. As Brock continued flipping through generic shows, her patience wore thin. She swiped the remote from his hand and changed the channels herself, eyes glued to every pixelated image that flicked past. "I think I'm gonna be sick."

"Whatever happens, you'll survive this," he assured her, picking up an iPad resting on the arm of the leather sectional. "Keep looking. I'm going to search the web."

She resembled a woman possessed by madness as she clicked over and over, desperate to find an anchor who would explain everything they knew about the body.

Finally, mercifully, Brock announced, "Got it!"

She pounced against his side and gripped the tablet so it was situated between them.

Body found near Cave Junction identified as local treasure hunter

A body found on Wednesday morning near Oregon Caves National Monument and Preserve has been identified as David Jones, 58, of Holland, Oregon. Jones was a renowned historian and head of a team of treasure hunters known to locals as "The Treasured Ten."

Lieutenant Brenda Tauer with the Josephine County Sheriff's Office announced a report was made at 10:34 a.m.

of an adult male who appeared to have been deceased for a significant amount of time outside the Preserve. Officers arrived on scene at 10:47 a.m.

Lieutenant Tauer stated the cause of death is unknown, and an investigation is under way. She emphasized there are no safety concerns for the public at this time.

Something in the depths of Andy's mind sparked to life, crawling through her brain with the pace of a tortoise, but she couldn't put her finger on the source. Cradling her gnawing stomach, she slowly backed away.

The Treasured Ten. David Jones.

She knew these names.

"He was a treasure hunter," she heard Brock say, his voice oddly far away for someone standing so close by. "He must've had something to do with the diamond."

She nodded thoughtfully. It couldn't be a coincidence that the dead man had been a treasure hunter. Had he discovered the diamond, and she'd killed him for it?

"David Jones…that was David Bowie's real name," he said. "It's pretty generic otherwise." Lifting the tablet, he turned to her. "I have a feeling we might get somewhere if we can locate the rest of this 'Treasured Ten' group."

"He was a real pirate," Andy muttered.

Brock's fingers wrapped around her elbow. "What'd you say?"

Andy's dream from the other night replayed through her mind.

"Why did that man call you a pirate?"

"Because I hunt for treasure, darlin'."

"Are you a REAL pirate?"

"You bet your sweet little buns I am."

"I know…something," Andy told Brock, fisting her hands as she turned to face him. "I don't know if it's a memory from my childhood or something I heard in a movie, but there was a conversation with a man…a treasure hunter. He's been in my dreams a dozen times since I came to Astoria. And that name…David Jones…."

"Do you get the sense that you knew him?"

"Maybe." She gritted her teeth, fighting back angry tears. "Why was my life stolen from me, Brock? Why can't I remember anything?"

"It'll return one day," he said, setting the tablet

down to pull her into his arms. "We won't stop searching for the truth until it does."

She arched her head back to kiss him soundly, erasing any trace of her unease and heartache. He kissed her back with an unspoken promise to keep his word…to keep her safe. She reveled in the heat of his mouth and was eager to feel the tender comfort of his fingers, his lips. For all she knew, it had been years since she'd felt the touch of a man. She was desperate for any human connection, but more specifically, a connection with the man who had given her a chance when she hadn't had anywhere to turn.

He responded in kind, seeming starved for a taste of her as his skilled mouth nibbled at her neck, then a shoulder. Their lips met again in a fury of desperation and yearning. When his teeth tugged at her bottom lip, she released a satisfied sound that he must've taken for a cry the way he snapped back.

"Are you okay with this?" he whispered.

She nodded as she dragged her lips along his clean-shaven jaw. "Just don't stop. I need this. I need *you.*"

He scooped her into his arms and carried her out of the living room, their lips tasting and teasing the entire way to his bedroom.

He stripped off her pajama top and bottoms with

deft fingers, creating delightful goosebumps across her skin. She struggled to shimmy his sweat pants and boxers down his lean hips, giggling when he gave a helping hand.

As badly as she wanted to take her time to explore every crevice of his smooth muscles, to bask in the fresh scent of his golden skin, she couldn't wait any longer. She'd denied herself the pleasure of getting to know him this way for far too long. She sensed the reality of her situation was edging closer and feared her time on this earth would be limited.

The love of her life could be somewhere, eagerly waiting for her to return to him. Or, for all she knew, she was a virgin. Brock made her feel like one the way he took her with gentle ease and extreme care.

She could only hope they would live to enjoy another day of each other's company before the truth came crashing down around them.

CHAPTER 12

Brock

BROCK STARTLED awake with the faint sound of a pebble pinging against glass. The room was filled with a golden glow from the rising sun, and he was still naked, still fully entwined with the mysterious beauty who had finally let him in. He carefully released himself from Andy's sinewy limbs and slipped into the bedroom doorway, pausing to listen.

Another ping of a pebble breached the silence.

He glanced out the bedroom's wall of windows overlooking the bay. In the brilliance of the sunlight, he discovered the source of the sound. Two small, perfectly round holes breached the double panes of tempered glass.

Those weren't pebbles, he decided with equal clarity and alarm.

They were bullet holes.

Brock dove down to the floor and Army-crawled back toward the king-sized bed. On the side opposite the windows, he slithered up along the mattress and cupped a firm hand over Andy's mouth. Her green irises widened with alarm. He brought a finger to his lips and tilted his head backward, motioning for her to join him on the floor. She slipped down to his side with the sheet clutched in her hand, covering a fair portion of her nakedness.

"Someone's shooting at us," he whispered with his lips pressed up against her ear. "Where's the gun?"

She released a calming breath. "In the nightstand on the other side of the bed."

He quietly growled with discontent. The other side was exposed by the flank of floor-to-ceiling windows. Reaching over his head, he slid his cell phone down from the other floating nightstand and entered his password before handing the phone to Andy. "Text Knox, tell him we're under fire by a sniper, then get dressed. I'm going to grab the gun in case they come inside."

"They're here for the diamond," she told him, already scrolling through his apps. "They'd be stupid to kill us before we handed it over."

"Tell them that." He leaned in to kiss her softly. "Stay alert. We don't know who we're dealing with."

She nodded, the glow of his phone lighting her face as she quickly drafted a message with her thumbs. As he watched her, his heart did a funny little flip in his chest. He was falling way too hard for her and couldn't bear the thought of her getting hurt.

He crawled back around the bed, hearing another ping of a bullet overhead right as he wrapped his hands around the pistol. The master bedroom was positioned over the rocks at an angle so the shooter could either be in a neighbor's house or on the water. Either way, he worried someone else might get hit by a stray bullet.

He laid down and wiggled into the sweats he'd been wearing in the night before hurrying over to where Andy was already dressed in the pajamas he'd stripped her out of hours earlier.

"Knox is on his way," she whispered, handing his phone back to him.

He set the gun down and quickly typed out another message to his buddy.

Alert the Coast Guard. Shots might be coming from the water.

• • •

Andy took the gun from the floor between them and slipped it into her waistband like it was second nature to carry it there. "What's our plan?"

"Unless they breach the house, we wait in the pantry until Knox arrives. It's on the other side of the house, and the entrance is hidden." He motioned for her to follow on hands and knees into the hallway.

While passing the tall front door made entirely of glass, he cursed himself for building a house that exposed in every room. He glanced over his shoulder to ensure Andy was close behind when there was a loud explosion of breaking glass behind them. He spun around to see a black steel battering ram gliding across the entry's hardwood floor in a pile of broken glass.

A second later, a man in tactical gear and a face mask stepped through the shattered front door, gun pointed directly at Brock's head. He opened his mouth, intending to tell Andy to run. She was already sailing through the air, blocking the man's aim and simultaneously firing her pistol.

His ears rang with the two gunshots at close range.

The man jerked back and fell to his knees.

Andy hooked her hand under Brock's elbow and lifted him to his feet. "Come on! There could be more coming!"

As Brock stood, he watched in shock as the intruder sputtered blood with a hand held to his throat. Although he was wearing a Kevlar vest, Andy's two shots had landed inside his shoulder and neck. Either she had excellent luck, or she was a skilled marksman.

They sprinted through the house toward the kitchen. Brock pushed on the hidden pantry door and motioned for her to enter first. The automatic fluorescent lights flickered on over their heads as he closed the door behind them, revealing the shamefully bare shelves that came with the life of a bachelor.

Andy squared up before him and touched his face with a tentative smile. "Are you okay?"

"Who the hell are you?" he demanded, blinking rapidly. Seeing her in action was like watching a scene straight from *Tomb Raider*.

"Apparently, I'm good with a gun." Her face paled with the idea. "Do you still believe I'm not a killer? What if I killed David Jones?"

He pulled her into his arms and dropped a kiss in her hair as police sirens screamed in the distance. "It's gonna be okay," he assured her, even though he wasn't entirely convinced it was true anymore.

"What do we do about the diamond?"

"We'll take it with us."

She drew back to look him in the eye. "Where are we going?"

"Back to where this all started."

As Brock answered a call from Knox, he watched Andy interact with Rio, an old friend who was a retired pilot for the Coast Guard. Her smiles were stiff, but her gaze remained friendly as they carried on in the center of the private airplane hanger. While Brock didn't think there was any reason to fear her at that point—after all, she had saved his life—he couldn't shake the shock of witnessing her in action. He wanted to believe she was some kind of officer of the law to justify her expertise, but the idea seemed implausible. They would've heard something in the news by that point.

"I just got off the phone with your sister," Knox reported. "She said someone broke into the apartment above the brewery and tore the place to shreds. They were clearly eager to find something. Since Christina spent the night in the county jail, it's safe to say it wasn't her."

Brock closed his eyes, thankful Andy had agreed to stay at his place. "Any updates on the shooter?"

"The Coast Guard found an abandoned fishing

boat in your bay that had been reported as stolen early this morning," Knox reported. "Seems likely it was used by the shooter or an accomplice. Your intruder is still unconscious. They're prepping him for surgery to remove the bullet in his neck, but the surgeon isn't optimistic that he'll pull through."

"Any idea who he is yet?"

"That could be a problem. His fingerprints have been…*altered*."

"Altered how?"

"Shaved off."

With a shaky breath, Brock stabbed his fingers through his hair. Who *were* these people shooting at them? They clearly weren't messing around.

"I don't know what your hot little girlfriend has going on," Knox told him, "but this isn't some loser boyfriend we're dealing with. This guy was a professional."

"Maybe the boyfriend hired a professional."

"You're full of shit," Knox snapped. "You've always been like a brother to me, Resner. I thought we were honest with each other. Don't make me throw your ass in the clink for withholding evidence. What the hell's going on? First, Andy goes after the DA; now she executes a man with perfect aim."

"It was a home invasion. She shot the intruder before he shot me."

"With a gun she claims she pitched over the cliff when she panicked and realized what she had done? Come on, Brock. I wasn't born yesterday. Where'd she get the gun in the first place? How was she so quick to defend you? What does she have hidden in her apartment?"

"It's complicated."

Knox huffed with a frustrated sound. "What about that dead treasure hunter they found near Cave Junction? Seems to be a big coincidence you met her as she was fleeing from there. Is she involved with him, too?"

"Don't make me lie to you."

"Why do you insist on protecting her?" Knox demanded.

"Because there's no one else. I'm all she has."

"Don't tell me you're falling in love with her, brother. She's beginning to make Christina look harmless."

Brock took a deep breath, determined not to spew too many lies to his buddy. He couldn't deny he felt a deeper connection with Andy after they'd slept together. He just couldn't be sure how deep that connection went. It seemed wrong to want more from her when there were still so many unanswered questions. Would he be able to love her even if she turned out to be a murderer?

Was there really such a thing as justifiable homicide?

"Christ, Resner!" Knox scolded with a roar. "I'm beginning to think that fat cash of yours has fried your brain!"

"Trust me on this one, Knox. I know what I'm doing, alright?"

"Fine, but you better line up a good defense attorney for your girl and keep her close to your place. If this guy dies, she could be facing some serious charges."

"We're taking a quick trip out of town," Brock confessed. It was better to break the news to his buddy that they were leaving rather than him to find out another way. "She's pretty shaken up, so I thought taking her away would be a good idea. We're going to Portland…should be back in a day or two."

"Not the best idea under the circumstances, but I guess I can understand. As long as I have your word that you're going to Portland and not taking her to Canada to make a grand escape, I'm okay with it."

Brock refused to consent to giving his word when it was yet another fabrication. He compromised with, "No trips to Canada. I promise."

"Keep your phone close in case more of her old buddies decide to pay you a visit. I may not agree with all this, but you're still my brother. I'd take a bullet for you, no questions asked."

"Ten-four, brother."

Brock ended the call, annoyed to discover Rio was making one of his signature moves on his girl by kneading her nearest shoulder. The guy easily had twenty years on her but was known for wooing women of all ages.

"We're all set to go," Brock announced, slipping his phone into his pocket as he snagged his backpack off the concrete floor and started for them. Although they weren't sure how long they'd be away, Andy had packed the necessities for an overnight visit, including one change of clothes for each of them. Brock acknowledged it was incredibly optimistic to believe they'd find the answers she needed that quickly.

Andy took a long stride from Rio to stand at Brock's side. "Rio was just telling me about his time served with the Coast Guard. Sounds like he's assisted in some pretty harrowing rescues."

Despite being annoyed with Rio's flirting, Brock threw his friend a grateful smile. He respected any veteran and regretted that he'd never served himself. "He's a good egg."

"Brock mentioned you had a nine mil," Rio told

Andy. He handed her a box of ammunition and winked. "Just in case."

Andy's beautiful eyes showed uncertainty when she met Brock's gaze. "Let's do this."

He pulled her in close and brushed his lips over her temple. "Breathe, babe. Everything's going to be alright." He vowed to continue telling himself that until it became true, no matter how long it may take.

CHAPTER 13

Andy

ANDY FELT she'd been holding her breath throughout the helicopter ride as they touched down in Cave Junction. Going back to the place where her nightmare began felt akin to stepping into a field of land mines. She had no idea who or what they would discover, or whether her actions would be vindicated. How she reacted to the intruder had rattled her to the core. She was more convinced than before that she was a criminal, and their search for the truth would end with total chaos. Maybe even a lifetime in prison.

When Rio announced they could debark the helicopter and Brock climbed down to offer his hand to her, she feared she'd vomit up the pickles and boneless wings they'd ordered the night before. Although the fall temperature was mildly warm, violent chill.

"Are you okay?" Brock shouted over the the slowing propellers, his eyes heavy with con

"Don't know," she replied honestly, wrapping hair into a makeshift ponytail to protect it from surge of wind. She glanced around the empty fi adjacent to the runway, eyeing the shadowy moun tains with unease. "I'm starting to wonder if coming here was a mistake."

"This will all be over soon, and we can move forward with our lives." Brock swept his lips over hers before moving his mouth to her ear. "I'm going to settle up with Rio. I'll meet you in the car."

A black sedan waited at the edge of the runway. Andy could see a man in the driver's seat and decided she wouldn't take any chances. Since Brock had made all of the arrangements for their trip by phone, she wasn't sure who they could trust. Anyone they met in Cave Junction was a potential threat.

She folded her hands over her waist, feeling comforted by the sharp press of the diamond's points against her abdomen. For weeks, she'd had her eye on a small belt bag at Skye's boutique and had asked Brock to stop by there on their way out of town so she could buy it. Secured beneath one of Brock's flannels several sizes too large on her, the bag was undetectable. Still, she felt exposed, like a walking target.

She stood a few yards away from Rio and Brock, watching as they wrapped up a conversation before shaking hands and patting each other on the backs. Andy gave Rio a small wave before he climbed back into the helicopter. With the backpack slung over his shoulder, Brock caught up to Andy, took her hand, and threaded their fingers together.

"So what's it like having all these resources at your disposal?" she asked as they started for the car. "Are you used to being rich by now, or does it sometimes still weird you out?"

"I've taken a private jet down here a few times when it was necessary to check in with my satellite brewery. My accountant pushed me to do it, said I needed a legitimate write-off." He opened the sedan's back door and motioned for her to enter. "Otherwise, I don't normally indulge in frivolous things."

"Your sister said you helped her quite a bit—financially and otherwise."

"I'd be a jerk if I didn't use my money for something good."

As he verified their destination with the driver, she laughed. "I don't think you have it in you to be a jerk in general."

Brock held her hand on the 15-minute drive to the rental, obsessively stroking his thumb over her fingers. She wasn't sure if he was attempting to comfort her or himself. The winding roads surrounded by dense pine trees triggered the memory of waking beside the dead man. She closed her eyes and thought of the man's face, his name. *David Jones.* Was his group, this "Treasured Ten," behind the shooting? Maybe they were a gang of criminals, and she had recovered the stone with pure intentions.

After passing through the small town, their driver parked at the curb in front of a modest cedar cabin. Brock paid the driver before they slipped out onto the sidewalk. As Brock started for the rental's front door, Andy's eye caught on a flyer stapled to a nearby light pole. Her heart stilled. She was so accustomed to seeing herself with dark hair that the blonde in the picture could've been a stranger. Not only that, her expression was severe and stiff. She ripped the paper off the pole to study it closer.

MISSING PERSON

VELORA KLEIN

Last seen on July 30th outside of Cave Junction

wearing a blue sweatshirt and jeans. Age 28, green eyes, blond hair, 5'7" and 120 pounds.

A website address and a number to call with any information were listed at the bottom.

She sucked in a shallow breath.

Her name was Velora Klein.

Why didn't it sound at all familiar?

"It's me," she whispered, blindly passing the flyer to Brock.

With a strained look, his gaze passed back and forth between Andy and the flyer. She sensed he knew as well as she did that everything would change once they called the number listed.

"At least now we know your name, but it could still be some kind of setup," he decided. "Maybe I should call the number with your burner phone, see if they sound legit before we decide to do anything else."

"Let's visit the website first."

Brock switched the internet browser on his phone to incognito mode and typed in the address. A video popped onto the screen. Andy leaned over Brock to hit play. A deeply tanned man in his early 30s began to speak in the video. He was well-built with a square jaw, thick jet-black hair, and dark brown eyes that shone with desperation beneath thick eyebrows. He wore a sleeveless T-shirt that exposed his thick biceps, showcasing dozens of colorful tattoos.

A flutter arose in Andy's stomach. Something about the attractive man triggered a familiar feeling. She *knew* him.

"Velora Klein has been missing since July thirtieth," the man said in a gravely deep voice, his gaze unblinking as he stared into the camera. "She was last seen at a gas station twenty miles south of Cave Junction wearing a blue zip-up hoodie, blue jeans, and tan hiking boots." After he repeated her physical attributes listed on the flyer, his eyes glistened with unshed tears. "Lor, if you're watching this, please come home." His voice cracked a little when he continued. "We all love you, and we're worried sick. If you can access a phone, at least call me and let me know you're safe."

When the video ended, Andy felt as if she'd been drenched in cold water. That voice…those eyes…they sparked a distant memory that was too hazy, too far away to grasp. What role did the man play in her life? Was he a relative? A lover?

Brock cleared his throat. "Either that guy's really broken up about your disappearance, or he's an exceptional actor." He regarded her with the same level of uncertainty she was feeling. "Did he look familiar?"

"Maybe a little," she admitted. When his expression tightened as if in pain, she touched one side of his jaw. "Don't freak out yet. For all we know, he's my brother. He said, 'We all' love you. He could be speaking on behalf of himself and my parents."

His gaze darkened. "Or he's your husband, referring to himself and your children."

On a gasp, Andy spread a hand over her firm abs. She hadn't noticed any stretch marks, and she didn't have the slightest inkling that she'd once carried a life inside her. "Children? That's something a mother would never forget...right?" She shuddered, realizing that she could have little ones who desperately needed their momma while she was messing around in Astoria. "I mean, don't you think if I had given birth, it's something I would know?"

Brock's eyes skirted away from her. "I'm not sure what to believe at this point."

She sensed there was so much more he wanted to say as he turned his back to her and continued toward the house. She hurried to catch up with him, watching thoughtfully as he entered a passcode from his phone into the door's digital lock. No matter the reality of her situation, she was convinced Brock was too good of a man for someone like her. As he opened the rental's front door, she wrapped her fingers around his wrist.

"I wouldn't blame you if you wanted to leave, Brock. This has become too complicated. I won't take it personally if you return to Astoria without me."

Jaw clenched, he turned to face her. "What if you find out you are, in fact, married to that guy?"

"I don't know him," she answered, lifting one shoulder. "I'm not going to brush you off for a stranger who doesn't mean anything to me when you mean more than I'm willing to admit." She stood on her toes to brush her lips over his cheek, then rested her forehead against his jaw. "You took me in like a stray dog—gave me a place to stay when I had nothing. After I *stole* from you. That's not something I could ever forget."

He let out a long sigh and dropped his head. "There's no way I'm leaving you here by yourself when it's clear someone is willing to kill you for that diamond." His fingers slid beneath the hair on the back of her head, tilting it back so she was facing him. The fierce look he gave her erupted goosebumps along her arms and warmed her belly. "You mean something to me too. That's why I can't make any promises I'll be able to keep my shit together if we discover you're involved with someone. I won't give you up to another man without a fight."

Their mouths met for a heated kiss. Brock pushed his shoulder into the open door, and they stumbled through the threshold while still connected, tugging at each other's clothing until they were both naked in the center of a room. Andy didn't bother looking around to acknowledge their new surroundings. She was too focused on the kindhearted man kissing her with a desperation that made it feel as if he needed to be with her because the world was about to end.

She knew exactly how he felt.

CHAPTER 14

Brock

ANDY PERCHED on the edge of the rental's microfiber couch across from Brock, knees bouncing as she watched him dial the number listed on the flyer. They both stared at the burner phone on the coffee table between them, its dull rings amplified on speakerphone cutting through the ominous silence.

As soon as the call connected, Brock stated, "I'm calling with some information about Velora Klein."

"Do you know where she is?" the same deep voice from the video asked.

"She's safe," Brock assured him. "But she's in danger. Someone shot at her this morning."

"Goddamn it! *Where is she*?" the man demanded forcefully.

"Where are *you*?" Brock countered. "If she decides

it's safe, she'd like to meet you in a place of her choosing."

"Listen, asshole. I'm not playing games with you. Who the hell are you? If I find out you hurt her—"

"She's in good hands. I won't let anything happen to her." He wanted to add, "You have my word," but he had yet to decide if the man and his motivations were authentic. "What's your name?"

"Trevor."

"Trevor *what*?"

"Trevor Holiday. What's yours?"

Andy shook her head and shrugged, indicating the name wasn't ringing any bells.

Brock heaved a small sigh of relief. At least they didn't share a last name. "Do you know why someone would be after Velora?"

"I have a pretty good idea."

Andy and Brock's gazes met. "It'd be helpful if you shared that idea," he told Trevor.

"Not necessary. She knows."

When Andy made an exasperated face, Brock said, "Humor me."

"She disappeared with something valuable."

Does he know about the diamond? Brock wondered as Andy's eyebrows lifted. Would it make him a friend or a foe if he knew? "How did she acquire it to begin with?"

"Why don't you ask her?"

Brock remained silent. Once they'd decided to make the call, Andy had agreed it was best to try to extract as much information as possible without letting the stranger know the extent of her situation. At least until they were sure he could be trusted.

"How do you know Velora?" Brock asked, cringing at every mention of her real name. To him, she'd always be Andy.

"She's an extremely close friend—more like family." Trevor's voice was hard and impatient. "She means the world to me, so I'd suggest you return her unharmed unless you want to find out what I'm capable of."

"Just a friend?" Brock pushed, swinging his gaze over to Andy. "I get the sense she's more than that to you."

"My relationship with her is none of your damn business."

If he only knew, Brock thought bitterly. "You mentioned in the video that you 'all' loved her. Who else were you referring to?"

"Her other friends. We're a close crew. She's lived with nearly all of us at one point in her life."

"Who was David Jones?"

Trevor made a noise deep inside his throat. "Now I know you're full of shit. If Velora was with you and she's unharmed, she could tell you herself."

Brock wasn't sure it was a good thing that Andy had known the dead man. "What about the Treasured Ten?"

Trevor paused. "Where's Velora? What have you done with her? Dammit! Either *tell me,* or this conversation is over!"

"I'm right here," Andy answered.

Brock briefly closed his eyes. It was too soon for her to get involved in the conversation. Trevor had yet to prove he knew her the way he claimed.

"Lor?" Trevor cried with strangled laughter. "Is that really you?"

"It's me," she assured him.

"Lor, *babe,* where the hell have you been? Where are you?"

Brock's skin crawled with the affectionate way Trevor used the term "babe." Even if they were only friends, as Trevor claimed, it seemed apparent he hoped for something more. Brock understood precisely how a man would feel that way.

Reading Brock's uneasy expression, Andy squeezed his hand as she answered Trevor. "We're in Cave Junction."

"Are you *kidding* me?" Trevor yelled. "Have you been here this whole time?"

"No. It's a long story."

"Tell me where you are. I'm coming to get you."

"I can't do that. Like my friend told you, I'm in danger. I shot and possibly killed a man."

"They'll send more men, Lor, and you know it! Tell me where you are so I can protect you!"

"We'll meet you at Resner Brewery in twenty minutes," she told him. "Come alone and bring proof that we know each other. Don't tell anyone I'm in town or the meeting's off, and you won't hear from me again."

Brock shook his head as she touched the screen to end the call. "I'm not convinced this is a good idea."

Stone-faced, she shrugged. "I guess we'll find out."

Once inside his brewery, Brock met with the manager to let her know he was visiting some friends in town and didn't want to be disturbed. Then he returned to Andy with two steins of blueberry beer, and they claimed a table in the far rear corner where they could keep an eye on everyone who entered. It was relatively quiet in the time gap between lunch and dinner, with only a handful of tourists indulging in appetizers and brew. Andy remained cool and collected at his side, sipping on the fruity ale like she was waiting on an old friend. Brock wanted to clear the place out to eliminate any potential problems. What if this "Trevor" was only putting on an act?

Several minutes later, the jacked-up guy from the video rushed through the front door in a pair of joggers and a thick gray hoodie with bright white sneakers. Brock wasn't sure if he felt threatened by the guy because of his intimidating bulk and stature or because he could be the center of Andy's universe.

Brock leaned closer to Andy. "Keep that gun handy."

Once Trevor spotted them, he rushed over to wrap Andy in a tight embrace. "Thank God you're okay," he said, lifting her feet off the floor. "I've never been so relieved to see someone."

Andy remained unresponsive in his arms, gaze placid. Although Brock wanted to save her, he remained silent. He sensed the poor guy, whoever he was to her, had legitimately been devastated by her disappearance. As Andy reclaimed her seat, Trevor lowered to the chair on her other side and draped an arm behind her as if claiming his property. His dark eyes sharpened on Brock. "I'm assuming you're the guy that called. You're lucky I don't knock you out for half of what you said."

"This is Brock," Andy told him, taking Brock's hand in hers. "We're together, so take it easy on him."

Trevor's upper lip trembled with a surge of anger. "Since when have you become involved in romantic relationships? You've never had the time nor the interest. You're essentially asexual."

Brock chuckled when Andy's eyes popped wide, and her lips lagged open. "You sure about that?" he asked Trevor.

Anger radiated from Trevor as his dark eyes shifted back and forth between Brock and Andy. "You saying you've slept together?"

"Not that it's any of your business, but maybe I was just waiting for the right guy to come along," Andy replied, her voice calm and confident.

Brock wanted to drag her into his lap and continue where they'd left off earlier in the rental. Especially since Trevor had essentially confirmed she was unattached. Once things settled down, Brock intended to ask her to move in with him. He couldn't have cared less about having an expensive house or nice things. He only wanted someone with her warmth and sincerity to bring meaning and excitement into his otherwise sterile life.

Head tilted, Trevor eyed Andy with a slight scowl. "You've changed. And I mean more than just your hair color. I'm not sure I'm okay with it."

"I don't care what *you're* okay with," Andy snapped. "I've been through a lot. I disappeared because I was involved in some kind of accident. I hit my head pretty hard. My memory's been a bit hazy since, so I need your help filling in a few blanks."

"That would explain your involvement with this clown," Trevor mumbled, throwing Brock a murderous glare. He studied Andy once again. "What kind of accident? Were you in the hospital?"

"None of that matters. I just want a few questions answered, like who are the Treasured Ten, and who's after me?"

"Are you messing with me?" Trevor asked, his voice nearly an octave higher. When Andy shook her head, he let out a low whistle. "You must've really hit your head *hard*." Frowning, he leaned back with a hand feathering through his dark hair. "You've practically been a part of the Treasured Ten since birth. Do I seriously have to explain this to you? I mean, you really don't remember anything about it?"

Brock's gut plummeted. *Since birth?* What kind of group was Andy caught up in? Was it some kind of a cult?

"Like I said, I hit my head." Andy lifted her hands at her sides. "Please indulge me. Pretend I'm a complete stranger."

Trevor looked tentatively at Brock before carefully

sweeping his gaze across the brewery. He then leaned in closer to the table and lowered his voice. "We're a group dedicated to hunting for treasure. We turn some of our discoveries over to the government, profit off the finder's fees. Others we're able to keep under the 'finders keepers' law."

"What kind of people are involved in this group?" Brock probed.

Through a clenched jaw, Trevor replied, "Our team's specialties range from elite military to a local historian. There's also a geologist, a history professor, and a pair of archeologists. A millionaire funds our expenses until we're paid."

Andy blinked several times, seeming to absorb the information before speaking. "What's my specialty? What do I bring to the team?"

Trevor appeared especially disturbed by her questions. His eyes cast downward as he shifted in his chair. "Lor, *come on*. Have you seen a doctor about this condition of yours?"

"No, but I'm pretty sure it's dissociative amnesia. It's a condition that can be triggered by trauma or stress."

Trevor gave her a scolding look. "You and me... we're the tactical brains and brawn of the crew." He then let out a blunt, incredulous laugh. "We're both former Army Rangers…met in Ranger School. It's where you recruited me."

Andy exchanged a surprised, wide-eyed look with Brock and sat back in her chair. Brock sensed there was something noble about her and wasn't nearly as shocked to hear the truth as she appeared to be. To be honest, he was shamelessly turned on. He knew she was extraordinary once he'd witnessed her swiping his credit card with the ease of a blackjack dealer. More than anything, however, he was disturbed to discover she'd earned the prestigious title and didn't remember anything about the process. He wished he would've forced her to see a doctor even though she'd refused.

First slugging down the remainder of her ale, Andy paused to think, then sucked in an unsteady breath. "W-who's after me?" she stuttered.

"His name is Vladimir Babanin," Trevor whispered. "He's a Russian billionaire even more obsessed with finding Peg Leg Paulsgrave's blue diamond than we've ever been. He has endless resources, Lor. He won't stop coming after you—*us*."

All at once becoming pale, Andy wrapped an arm over her stomach as if she had a belly ache. Brock assumed she was instinctively protecting the diamond. He was beyond dismayed to learn someone with that kind of power and wealth had put a target on his woman's back. He was equally frustrated, knowing there most likely wasn't a damn thing he could do about it. Men with that degree of riches were invincible and could make anything happen.

"Peg Leg Paulsgrave?" Brock asked.

The way Trevor flinched with the sound of Brock's voice, it seemed as if Trevor had momentarily forgotten he wasn't alone with Andy. "He was the pirate who first stole the diamond from a sea captain back in the early seventeen hundreds."

With a shake of her head, Andy gripped the table, bracing herself. "Where's your proof we know each other that I asked you to bring?"

Trevor produced a smartphone from his pocket and swiped his finger over the screen a few times before handing the device to Andy. Brock leaned over her shoulder to study the picture of a group of men and women standing near the mouth of a cave, arms linked around each other's shoulders. By his quick count, there were only nine in all. A blonde Andy, maybe a handful of years younger than the one Brock knew, stood front and center among them in khaki pants and a chambray shirt, hair slicked back into a neat bun, lips slightly curled at the edges in a modest smile. Although she stood beside a baby-faced

Trevor, her head rested on the shoulder of the older man on her other side.

Andy zoomed in on the man and showed the picture to Trevor. "Is that David Jones?"

Trevor glanced at it and barked out a laugh. "You can't be serious."

"That's him, right?" she bit out impatiently. "The man they found dead in the forest?"

"Lor," Trevor scolded with a shake of his head. "David Jones was your father."

CHAPTER 15

Andy

ONCE EN ROUTE back to the rental, Andy wasn't sure how to feel. She couldn't wrap her head around the fact that she had been a soldier, even if it did seem logical considering she had the skillset to go along with it, so she chose not to dwell on it any longer. It was unquestionably tragic she had lost her father, and she assumed that was the trauma that had stilted her memory. Quite honestly, it made her feel a little empty. But she couldn't remember anything about David Jones besides the memories that had come to her in her sleep. How could she properly mourn a man she didn't remember?

"Why did that man call you a pirate?"

Her question was met with a deep, joyful chuckle. "Because I hunt for treasure, darlin'."

"Are you a REAL pirate?"

The man cupped her chin and grinned. "You bet your sweet little buns I am."

The content of her dreams over the last several weeks finally made sense. They were memories of her childhood that her mind refused to let go of, no matter the circumstances. She must've learned of her father's adventures at a young, naive age.

Trevor parked his black Hummer on a quiet road about three-quarters of a mile away from the rental. "It's best if we walk from here," he told them. "We can wait it out a little, ensure we're not being followed."

Nodding, Andy slid out from the passenger's side and waited for Brock to join her from the backseat. He appeared oddly unfazed by everything they'd learned about her past when he cocooned her inside his arms, cradling her head.

"How are you dealing with everything?" he asked, dropping a kiss inside her hair.

She closed her eyes and let out a shaky sigh. In any other situation, she could've stayed in the safety of his arms forever. "It's exhausting to hear about a life I don't remember."

"Just remind me never to sneak up on you. I'd hate to learn firsthand whatever lethal moves you acquired in Ranger school."

Her bright laughter dulled into a frustrated groan. The last thing she wanted was for him to suddenly become afraid of her…even if she was becoming a little frightened of herself and what other unknowns were ahead or what she could do.

The trio cut through the edge of the forest and stood behind a wall of large boulders for a short period before Trevor deemed it safe to continue.

Once Brock unlocked the rental's front door, Trevor withdrew a Glock from his waistband. "You two wait out here. I'm going to make a quick sweep inside."

Irritation rushed through Andy. She didn't need a man to come to her rescue. The only thing she wanted from Trevor was more answers. He had stopped their conversation after revealing David Jones was her father, claiming it would be better to speak somewhere private.

Trevor reappeared in the doorway, dipping his chin. "All clear."

"My hero," Andy muttered, stepping in past him.

"There's the Velora I know," he said with a chuckle.

"I go by Andy now," she told him with a dark look. "I'd rather you didn't call me anything else."

"Whatever you say," Trevor huffed out.

Andy and Brock sat on the couch together, watching wearily as Trevor closed the door and put his Glock away. Andy felt the cool metallic press of her own pistol tucked into the back of her jeans and wondered how long it would be until she was forced to use it again.

"Why is my last name different than my father's?" she asked Trevor, motioning to the flyer still resting on the coffee table.

"Your parents never married," he answered. "Your mom gave you her last name when you were born."

"What happened to my father? Did I have any reason to kill him?"

"Hell no," he assured her, lowering into the faded armchair across from the couch. "You've worshiped him your entire life. Your mom left him when you were five, said she was tired of his foolish adventures. You refused to go with her because you believed in your father's mission." When Andy gave him a cynical look, Trevor shook his head. "You'll just have to trust me on this, babe. There's no way you had anything to do with his death. Babanin's thugs must've killed him."

Brock's spine stiffened when Trevor once again called her "babe." It was also grating on her nerves, but she intended to address that later. "Do you know why I would've been in the forest with him?" she asked.

"For whatever reason, you must've recovered the diamond from the cave. They probably shot your father because he got in their way."

"Why didn't they kill me too?" *And why didn't they search me for the diamond?* she silently added.

Trevor shrugged. "That's a good question."

Pretending to stretch her back and adjust her position on the couch, Andy subtly retrieved the pistol from behind her and laid it in her lap. "You know, *babe,* it's funny that you haven't asked me what I did with the diamond."

Trevor's eyes skipped between her and the weapon. "What is this? What the hell are you suggesting?"

"It's an exceptionally warm day," she said, lifting her chin as she regarded his sweatshirt. "Why does it feel like you're trying to hide something?"

Trevor's entire body tensed. "What could I possibly be trying to hide?"

Laughing with sarcasm, she winged a brow. "Are you wearing a wire? Or maybe there's a certain tattoo you don't want us to see."

"What? No!" He sprang to his feet and tugged the sweatshirt over his head, revealing two inked sleeves and an impressively cut physique. He slowly rotated each of his arms, giving Brock and Andy time to study his ripped biceps and forearms. The tattooed designs were intricate and finely detailed, some on the darker side—like a large skull and a snake surrounding a dagger—others whimsical, like a mermaid and a pirate ship. When she leaned back, satisfied he wasn't hiding anything, he scowled at her. "I was lifting at the gym when your *buddy* called. The sweatshirt was the first thing I grabbed from my gym bag. I was in a hurry to see you. You happy?"

Brock grunted. "A pirate ship seems like an interesting choice, all things considered."

Trevor regarded him with a scowl. "What do you want me to say, man? We're treasure hunters."

"There were only nine people in the picture you showed us," Brock pointed out. "Where's the tenth?"

"Gunnar likes to stay low on the radar," Brock told him, rubbing a hand over his head. "He extracts insider information for us in a way that isn't exactly legal."

Lost in thought, Andy narrowed her eyes at

Brock. "How do I know you didn't go rogue and shoot my father so you could keep the diamond for yourself?"

Trevor released a tight, unamused laugh. "Lor—I mean *Andy*—this is ridiculous. You saw the picture of us together, right? I'm your oldest friend. I know you better than anyone. That's why I didn't ask you about the diamond. I knew you would only get spooked if I brought it up before I'd earned your trust. I wanted to make sure you'd stick around so I could help keep you—and presumably the diamond you're carrying—safe."

Still skeptical, she leaned back and crossed her arms, stare unyielding on Trevor as he threw the sweatshirt back over his head and shimmied it around his lean waist. Even though she was more drawn to Brock's unassuming good looks, there was no denying Trevor was more handsome than the average man. She couldn't help wondering if he possessed a personality flaw that prevented her from reciprocating his attraction to her in the past.

"How did your crew know about the diamond to begin with?" Brock asked him. "I searched the web on the way back here and couldn't find a single mention of Peg Leg Paulsgrave."

"*Andy's* father was a local historian. He first heard about the diamond a few years back when one of his old buddies got drunk and repeated the story of a distant relative rumored to have been a pirate. Your father convinced a British professor specializing in eighteenth-century history to help him piece together the story of the lost blue diamond. They've kept a tight lid on their findings, knowing if the media got ahold of their story, there'd be thousands of whackos attempting to search for it." Trevor's eyes flipped back to Andy. "Emma's the newest member of our crew, but she's more of a mom to you than your birth mother."

Andy quirked a brow. "Where is she?"

"On her way back from England. When I told her you'd returned, she grabbed the first flight out."

She gritted her teeth. "Thought I told you not to tell anyone I was here."

"Doesn't matter," Trevor answered with a dismissive shake of her head. "She's family."

Brock grunted in a dissatisfied sound. "Where are the rest of the treasure hunters?"

"Most of them are scattered around the country. We do a lot of our research remotely these days." He grinned at Andy. "But your father's closest buddy lives less than half an hour down the road. We can visit him if you'd like. We can even stop at the house you shared with your father—it's on the way."

Although Andy was dying to see where she lived

and maybe even get a sense of this former Army Ranger persona who hunted for treasure with her father and his friends, she snorted. "And be met by an ambush? No thanks."

Trevor threw his hands out. "I wouldn't hurt you in a million years! What's it going to take for you to trust me again?"

"Time," Andy decided with a shrug. "And more information. Let's start with the story my father was given about the diamond."

"I'll let your father tell you himself." He pulled his phone out from his pocket and pecked at the screen several times before passing it over to Andy. "He typed it out and sent it in an encrypted message to the rest of us."

Andy sat close to Brock, drawing strength from his warm body as she leaned in close so they could read the email together.

In 1710, Captain Thomas O'Malley received a treasure from the British King after rescuing the king's daughter from a band of violent pirates. One of O'Malley's men, a young pirate named Paulsgrave, stole the treasure and abandoned the ship, anchoring the ship's stolen rowboat outside Cave Junction. For days, Paulsgrave hid deep inside the caves along with the treasure he'd stolen from Captain O'Malley. Once O'Malley discovered the treasure was missing, he brought a fleet of his men after Paulsgrave to reclaim the booty. When O'Malley's men cornered Paulsgrave inside one of the caves, he allegedly plunged to his death, falling hundreds of feet into the abyss. O'Malley's crew was unable to locate Paulsgrave's body. All they could find was his wooden leg, broken to bits. Legend has it Paulsgrave kept something from the treasure on his person—a rare blue diamond he intended to give to Lady Margaret Elizabeth, the love of his life. And I think I've discovered the exact location of where he died.

"Sounds like the kind of outlandish fairytale you'd read in a children's book," Andy decided with a dubious shake of her head.

"You said nearly the exact same thing when you first read that email," Trevor informed her with a cocky grin. "Maybe you haven't changed as much as I thought."

"You're saying Andy's father somehow discovered the exact same cave where this Paulsgrave pirate was rumored to have died over three hundred years ago?"

"Not just her father. The entire crew. *Andy* and I

repelled down countless caves in the past several years. She's the one who discovered the diamond embedded inside a pile of stalagmite, so it was decided she'd have the honor of extracting it from the cavern." He tilted his head to one side as he studied Andy. "I'm trying to understand why you would've gone to recover the diamond the same day your father was murdered. We'd planned the extraction for the following week when Emma was stateside and the others could join us for a big celebration. You and I were taking turns guarding the entrance to the cave just in case someone had caught wind of our discovery."

Andy rose from the couch on wobbling legs and returned the pistol to her waistband. "I'll be right back," she told the two men. "I just need…a minute."

She relieved herself in the rental's small bathroom with a clawfoot tub and a retro linoleum floor before splashing cold water onto her face. She patted her skin dry and examined her spooked reflection in the mirror, trying to envision the kind of woman who would repel into a dark cave in search of hidden treasure. Why *had* she recovered the diamond on her own? Had *she* gone rouge for whatever reason, and her father had caught onto her plan?

I'd like to believe you're a good person with good inten-

tions, Brock had said to her. But what if he was wrong?

As she stepped into the hallway, a large hand sealed over her mouth from behind.

"Give me the diamond," Trevor rasped, his breath hot against her ear.

CHAPTER 16

Brock

WITH THE JARRING sounds of a commotion in the hallway, Brock sprang to his feet. He moved just in time to avoid becoming a target of the bullet that shattered the rental's bay window and ripped through the back of the couch.

"Shooter!" he called, racing toward the small bathroom. "Someone's—"

He froze in the hallway, finding Andy sprawled on her back on the floor with her legs coiled tightly around Trevor's torso, her arm hooked around his throat. Brock's heart thudded violently. He wanted to help but doubted he could restrain Trevor any better than she'd done. The man's face was a deep shade of red from fighting back. "What happened?"

"He tried to take the diamond!" Andy explained through tight breaths.

"Only because I spotted a sniper across the street! They must know you have it, so I figured it'd be better off with me!" Trevor countered, wrestling free. He rolled away from her and scrambled to his feet, straightening his clothing with an irritated look. "Damn, woman. You're still in top shape."

Brock offered a hand to Andy, assisting her to her feet. "We'll settle this later," he told them, throwing Trevor an angry glare. "We have to get out of here—*now.* If I hadn't heard you two fighting, I would've been taken out by the sniper. They took a shot through the bay window."

"We have to stash the diamond somewhere safe," Trevor decided, removing his gun and releasing the safety. "At least until we can contact the rest of the team and devise a plan."

Although Trevor kept the muzzle aimed at the floor, Brock felt uncomfortable and wished he possessed a weapon as well. How was he expected to protect Andy if this guy decided to betray them?

"First, we need to get out of here in one piece," Brock clarified in a show of dominance. "We can try the window overlooking the backyard." Still holding Andy's hand, he tugged her back toward the bedroom. He wasn't pleased to hear Trevor following close behind as he wasn't positive they could trust him. What if he had arranged for the shooter to take Brock out so he could get his hands on the diamond?

While Brock retrieved the backpack from the bed, Andy ran to the window, sliding the pane upward and kicking out the screen. She grabbed her pistol before giving Brock a lingering look of uncertainty. "I'm going to check to make sure it's safe before we all go." When she quickly swept her warm lips over his, he prayed it wasn't the last time.

It pained him to let his woman take the lead in such a perilous situation, but he nodded once to let her know he understood. After all, she was a former Ranger. "Be careful."

"Prick," Trevor grumbled behind him as she climbed through the open window. "Don't understand what she sees in you."

Brock wondered the same as they watched Andy race around the yard, darting behind thick trees and dense bushes that led into the forest. The knowledge of her past had given her more confidence. Either that, or bits of her muscle memory were beginning to return. He couldn't believe he'd become involved with a bonafide action hero. She eventually waved a hand through the air, motioning for the men to join her. Brock hurried out, eager to get her as far away from the shooter as possible.

They all three ducked as another shot whizzed past.

The shooter had found them.

"This way," Trevor whispered, breaching forest's edge.

Andy and Brock exchanged a quick, wide-eyed look before reluctantly starting after him. Brock only had a vague idea of the layout of the little town, and it was better to have Trevor ahead so he couldn't sneak up on them and attempt to take the diamond a second time. As they were forced to jump over fallen logs and zip around other debris in their path, Brock was grateful he at least stayed in decent shape to keep up with the other two.

When Trevor's black Hummer came into sight, Brock realized they had zig-zagged their way back to throw the sniper off their trail. Trevor tossed a set of keys at Brock. "You can drive. I want both hands free in case we're tailed."

"Where are we going?" Brock asked, hurrying to the driver's side.

"To *Andy's* place," Trevor explained while opening the backseat door for her.

"What if the shooters know where she lives?" Brock asked.

Trevor met his gaze as they slid inside the vehicle and closed the doors. "Her father became paranoid a few years back after he recovered his last multi-million dollar treasure, and it was stolen from their house. He had an underground passageway installed on the property's edge leading to a bunker out back. If someone's watching her house, they won't see us. The other team members are the only ones who know about the bunker."

As Brock started the engine, Andy poked her head in between them. "What if it's not this Russian billionaire that's shooting at us? What if someone else from our team has turned against us?"

"There's no way," Trevor told her. "Your father hand-picked everyone. He trusted each and every one of us with his life."

"Either way, we're being targeted and need to find somewhere safe," Brock added, glancing in Trevor's direction as he backed down the narrow road. "Which way do I turn?"

Fifteen minutes later, they were far from Astoria and back on a winding road flanked by massive pine trees. From the passenger's seat, Trevor pointed out a driveway entrance. "That's her house. Keep driving…it's just a little farther ahead."

A three-story mansion sat atop a grand hill in a

clearing of trees, stretching at least a hundred feet wide. The house was sided in rich red cedar planks and field rock in a neither outdated nor modern style. It perfectly blended in among its natural surroundings. Once Brock saw the monstrosity, he watched Andy's reaction in the rearview mirror. She darted to the window, eyes stretched wide as she placed her palm against the glass. "I lived there?"

"Your father was a very wealthy man," Trevor stated with a chuckle. "I suppose that now makes you a very wealthy woman…in addition to what you already have."

Another reason for there being a target on her back, Brock thought angrily. "It doesn't look at all familiar?" he asked her.

"No," she said with a huff, leaning back against the seat. "Hopefully, my belongings and whatever else is in that house will stir up some memories."

Brock followed Trevor's directions down a heavily wooded off-road trail covered in weeds. He struggled to follow the set of previous tracks embedded in the dirt. Andy and Trevor clung to the bars over their heads as the vehicle swayed and jolted down the bumpy path.

When they reached a mass of vines covering several large boulders, Trevor commanded, "Stop here." He glanced back to Andy in the backseat. "Sit tight until I'm certain it's safe."

Tapping his thumbs against the steering wheel, Brock watched him jump out of the vehicle and slip to the back. "What do you think about this guy?" he asked Andy. "Think he's someone we can trust?"

She stretched a leg over the center console with a heavy sigh and slid into the passenger's seat. "I mean he did try to take the diamond, but I don't think we have any other options."

"The only thing I'm certain of is that he has a serious crush on you."

"What are you worried about?" she teased with a twinkle in her eye. "I'm asexual, remember?"

Brock cupped one side of her jaw in his hand. "Let's take off, just the two of us. I can charter a private jet to anywhere you want. The Maldives, Bora Bora, Positano, you name it."

"As tempting as the offer may be, I feel like I have an obligation to my father now, even if I don't remember him or what kind of relationship we had." She set her hand over his and momentarily closed her eyes. "I have to find his murderer and bring them to justice."

"We've been shot at twice now, Andy. Who the hell knows how many people are eager to get their hands on that diamond? I don't like where this is headed." He pulled her close to press their foreheads together. "I just found you. I can't stomach the idea of losing you."

"You're not going to lose me," she promised, stroking her hand along his cheek.

She lowered her mouth to his, kissing him softly, tentatively. Then her lips moved with determination as she swept her tongue against his. He gripped her face with both hands and groaned. Why did she have to be so damned driven to see things through? Her bravery and determination were both maddening and the biggest turn-on he'd ever known.

Part of him wanted to toss the damn diamond over a cliff and throw her over his shoulder to get her the hell out of there. The possibility that Trevor was leading them into an ambush wasn't far from his thoughts, even though Andy's passionate kisses made it hard to concentrate on much of anything.

Andy drew back with tears glinting in her eyes and a faint smile crossing over her lips. "Don't tell Trevor, but I think I might be falling in love…with someone other than myself."

With a sharp chuckle, Brock drew her close for another searing kiss. As badly as he wanted to say the words back to her, there were still too many unanswered questions for him to admit his feelings. He had yet to utter those three words to a woman and didn't want his first time to be marred with heartache and regret.

A sharp knock on the passenger's window broke them apart. Brock laughed happily when catching a glimpse of Trevor's angry scowl before he turned away and motioned with a stab of his finger for them to exit the vehicle.

"I think you might be right about the crush thing," Andy said with a playful grin. "Let's go. I'm eager to check out my old bedroom with my new boyfriend."

They met in front of the SUV and joined hands before trailing after Trevor. He paused between the pair of boulders stretching at least ten feet over him and glanced over each of his shoulders before pushing the mass of vines to one side. They were secured to a mesh panel covering a stainless steel door. A thumbprint pad was mounted above its handle. When Trevor lifted his thumb, intending to unlock it, Brock gripped his shoulder. "Hold on. If this really is a bunker leading to Andy's house, her thumbprint should get us inside."

Trevor stood back and gave a broad sweep of his arm. "Go for it."

She released Brock's hand and pressed her thumb against the pad. A green light flashed on the pad, and the door lock clicked. Andy glanced back at Brock with a satisfied grin. "Good call, *babe*."

As she pushed on the handle, Brock nudged her aside. "This could still be a trap. Trevor's going in first."

Trevor rolled his eyes. "Whatever you say, man." He walked through the threshold and flipped a switch at his side, revealing a narrow room with cement walls.

The room was seemingly empty except for a shaggy-haired blonde man with a good couple of decades on the trio leaning against one of the walls. He wore a black button-down shirt with white pinstripes, blue jeans, and expensive black leather loafers. The thick gold chains around his neck and large gold rings on his fingers glinted in the bunker's faint light as he rolled a toothpick between his broad lips. Despite the gold-rimmed glasses he wore over fair blue eyes that reminded Brock of an 80s movie star, the guy gave off serious Brad Pitt vibes with a blend of masculine features and laid-back charm.

Brock feared the man's intentions as he started for them.

Andy reached for her gun.

CHAPTER 17

Andy

EYES ON ANDY, the man's expression crumpled with pain. He rushed forward to embrace her and kiss her head. "I'm so sorry about your daddy, darlin'."

Heart pounding, she quickly wiggled free from the man's hold. Although she was relieved he didn't seem to be a threat, she couldn't breathe in his nicotine stench a moment longer without gaging. She took a step back to study the man. He was old enough to be her father, yet he was boyishly handsome like a beloved celebrity. "Who are you?"

The man glanced back at Trevor before his sky-blue eyes returned to her. "Velora," he said with a stilted laugh and a confused shake of his head, "it's me. *Oswald*."

"She hit her head," Trevor told him in a dry,

unamused tone. "Says she has amnesia and wants us to call her Andy."

"Because I *do* have amnesia," Andy snapped. She crossed her arms and threw Trevor a threatening glare. "Who else knows I'm here?"

"The entire team is on their way," Oswald answered. "Well, what's left of it now that your daddy's gone. We were terrified they'd done away with you too, darlin'."

Andy rolled her hand between them. "*They* as in…"

"Vladimir Babanin," Trevor replied. "Like I told you."

Oswald removed the toothpick from his lips and frowned. "You really don't remember anything?"

"Not really," she confessed, tired of pretending otherwise.

Oswald hung his head and started for the exit at the far end of the hallway. "Let's head inside. This conversation will be easier to digest over a stiff drink."

A faint shimmer of familiarity swept through Andy as she took in the house's grand ceilings and rustic furnishings. It wasn't exactly that she felt at home, but she sensed she had certainly set foot in the same spot before as she sipped on one of the old-fashioned cocktails Oswald had mixed. Brock had passed, which Andy decided was probably wise, but she liked how the harsh burn of alcohol seemed to sharpen her senses.

Her father had clearly been an outdoorsmen. The house's interior was clad in a dizzying mix of different species of woods, mainly knotty pine. Stuffed elk, deer, and bighorn sheep adorned numerous walls. The remaining decor, spread across the grand living room with 15-foot ceilings consisted of antique fishing nets, rods, and crab traps. An overall musty scent tinged with pipe tobacco clung to the air as they lounged on worn, dark brown leather couches and matching arm chairs.

"I was your daddy's oldest friend," Oswald began with a wistful look before sipping on his drink. "We met at the movie theatre, believe it or not—bonded over our love for the Indiana Jones movies. Long before you came along, your daddy told me he wanted to become a treasure hunter like Indy—thought it was fated since they had the same last name and all. I laughed it off at first until he told me about some of the places he'd researched. This was all before the internet, of course, so he'd put a lot of time and energy into hitting up different libraries, courthouses, and historical societies. He became so well-educated on the area's history that he left his position as a county worker to become a bonafide historian for Cave Junction."

"Did you know my mother?" Andy asked.

"Sure did." With a laugh, Oswald shifted the toothpick between his lips. "Winona didn't much care for me hanging around with your daddy, especially after I started coming over to help him research our first hunt."

Andy sat forward on the couch at Brock's side. "Do you know where she is now?"

Oswald threw her a sad yet charming smile. "Sorry, darlin'. We didn't exactly exchange numbers after she took off in a huff."

"Do you," she began, stopping to eye Trevor wearily. "I mean…is there any reason I would've wanted to hurt my father?"

Oswald guffawed and clapped his knee like she'd just recited the world's most hilarious joke. "Now *that's* a good one!"

"Told you," Trevor muttered, his face buried inside his glass mid-drink.

"Still can't believe I have to remind you of these things, but you and your daddy were like two peas in a pod. The idea of such a thing is, well, unfathomable."

"You think Vladimir Babanin killed him?" Brock asked.

"I suspect so," Oswald answered with a firm nod. "That greedy bastard was on a power trip to recover the diamond. As much as we tried to keep the hunt under the radar, he's apparently more powerful than we know." He regarded Andy with a mournful shake of his head. "Must've been keepin' an eye on your daddy for a long time."

"Do you think someone from your team could've been helping him?" Brock pushed. "Anyone desperate enough for money to take a fat bribe from Babanin?"

Oswald squinted with suspicion. "Who're you again?"

"My boyfriend," Andy told him for the third time since they'd arrived. "Brock knows everything…at least everything I've been told."

"I don't think anyone on this team is desperate for anything," Oswald decided, leaning back in the armchair across from them. "We've all generated our own fortunes over the years. But who the hell knows. I don't trust everyone the way old Jonesy did."

"This place seems like an obvious target for anyone looking for Andy," Brock told him. "Is there somewhere more secure we can hide until we know our next move?"

Trevor grunted with a laugh. "I'd like to see someone try to break into this place. *Andy's* father had it locked down tight." He gestured to the sheets of steel covering the giant wall of windows. "You couldn't break through those with a grenade."

An unexpected wave of exhaustion swept over Andy. Between the break-in at Brock's and the bevy of information she'd absorbed about herself, she couldn't handle anything more. She leaned against Brock, ready to collapse. He slipped an arm around her and kissed the top of her head. "When are the others supposed to arrive?" she asked.

Oswald slugged back what remained of his drink and set the glass on the arm of his chair. "Emma's last flight arrives early tomorrow morning. The rest should follow soon after."

Andy grabbed Brock's hand and pulled him up when she stood. "I've absorbed enough for one day. I need a good night of sleep if I'm going to keep my wits about me." She turned to leave, then stopped to glance between the two strange men who claimed to play an important role in her life. "Where's my bedroom?"

Andy stepped inside the large suite ahead of Brock, taking it in with tight, uneven breaths. Not a single flash of familiarity came to her as her eyes swept back and forth over every nook and cranny. The room was neat and tidy, with very few hints that it was once lived in. More steel sheets covered several windows on the far end of the suite, and a blue velvet couch with downy cream pillows stretched beneath them. A stone fireplace faced a cedar canopy bed with a fluffy white comforter covered in more decorative pillows. Whether or not Andy had anything to do with the interior decorating, she had to admit the bed was rather welcoming. Then again, she suspected anything would look good at that point as she was exhausted.

On a nightstand next to the bed, a picture framed in silver took her breath away. She strode over to examine it, taking enough time so her brain could comprehend what she was seeing. Decked out in a camo uniform and a beret, Velora embraced David Jones as they flashed bright smiles. Her father was fit and handsome in a navy suit jacket over a Foreigner band t-shirt and blue jeans. They were both notably younger than in Trevor's picture of her and her father alongside the rest of the team.

Emotion tore through her throat. "Either Trevor has gone to great lengths to sell us a story, or he wasn't lying about the Ranger thing," she called out to Brock. "Here's proof."

He stepped in behind her, coiling his arms around her waist. "Damn. You were insanely hot in that uniform." Sighing, he set his chin on her shoulder. "I'm really sorry about your father. I should've said something sooner." He pressed a soft kiss against the nape of her neck. "This must be weird as hell for you to process."

"When will my memory come back?" she choked out through tears. "I'm tired of everyone else telling me what happened and what he was like. I want to rely on memories that I know to be true."

"Let's get you cleaned up and tucked in," Brock whispered, gently nudging her around. After she rose on her tiptoes to kiss him, he took her hand and led her through an open barn door beyond the grand bed. They both took a moment to gaze around the attached bathroom, noting the open stone shower with enough nozzles to accommodate an entire basketball team and the built-in bathtub with more than enough room for two. On one end, a deep walk-in closet stretched along three walls. Andy gasped when spotting several sparkling evening gowns hanging from a rack with high heels lined up on a shelf below. She couldn't imagine what occasion in rural Oregon would require her to don something so elegant.

"How was this my life?" she asked, mostly to herself.

"I don't know, but I hope there comes a day when I can see you in one of those dresses."

Brock kicked his shoes off to one side of the bathroom and then turned to unbutton her shirt with a tender look that she felt in the depths of her soul. When she'd more or less confessed that she was falling in love with him, he hadn't hinted that his feelings for her ran as deep, but she sensed they were there just below the surface. It was one of the few things she'd been sure of in the last several months.

Brock helped slip her sneakers off, then unbuttoned her jeans. She shifted her legs as he tugged them down her solid thighs and pulled the leg openings over each of her feet. On his way back up to her, he pressed tender kisses against her bare skin, igniting her desire to be entangled with him yet again. She briefly closed her eyes and buried her hands inside his curly dark hair while taking a steady breath. The odor of chemicals burned through her lungs.

"Someone recently cleaned in here," she whispered. "Seems a little odd, considering this place has sat empty for a good chunk of time."

"Maybe Oswald or Trevor have been keeping the place up," Brock decided. With Andy's doubtful look, he chuckled. "Okay. More likely a loyal cleaning lady."

His fingers released the clasp on the bag containing the diamond. She clenched her jaw as he slipped it off of her body. "What are we going to do with it?"

"This bedroom suite is massive," he decided, eyeing the closet. "We should be able to find a spot to stash it until we find something better."

Nodding, she took the bag from him and entered the walk-in closet. Unlike the rest of the house, the shelving unit was sleek and modern. Beyond the gowns, a variety of styles from casual sweaters and jeans to tailored sports jackets and skirts filled the hangers. There were enough accessories like scarves, belts, and purses to stock Skye's shop. She opened a set of shaker doors to find wigs of different lengths and colors arranged on mannequin heads, along with various glasses and hats. Maybe she hadn't been wrong when she'd once wondered whether or not she could've been a spy. Part of her must've required posing as different characters for different hunts. Had that been an idea she had come up with alone, or had her father groomed her to become overly paranoid and cautious? In all fairness, it seemed someone who knew about their activities was trying to kill her.

Leaning in to examine a shallow tray containing elaborate earrings and necklaces, she noticed a small, square sensor embedded inside the velvet material. She pressed her thumb against it, and the tray gave a mechanical wheeze before sliding back.

Inside a deeper velvet bin, a rainbow of jewels winked back at her.

"Uh, babe?" she called over her shoulder, struggling to draw in a calming breath. "I think you should see this."

Brock's bare feet padded against the tiled floor behind her for a moment before he took a deep inhale. "Holy...*whoa.* That's an impressive stash. Must be worth a couple million."

Her stomach sank. Was *she* a traitor? "Do you think the others know I've been holding onto these? What if I've kept this compartment a secret from everyone, including my father?"

"There's no way of knowing for sure, but it seems a good hiding spot for now. I would think if there was a traitor among you and they knew about this loot, they would've taken it by now.

"But what if—"

Brock sealed his mouth over hers while removing both her tank top and bra strap with one flick of his wrist. He then leaned down to brush his lips over the newly exposed skin. "We've done enough pondering for one day, Andy." He ran his nose alongside her cheek while tugging at her underwear. "Put the diamond inside there so we can focus on the one thing we're sure of—how much we both want to get naked and break in that giant bed."

Relief flooded her as her questions began to fade away. Jumping into that welcoming bed with him was undoubtedly one thing she could do without questioning herself.

CHAPTER 18

Brock

BROCK WOKE with a gradual sense of panic spreading through his chest. Although the steel covering the bedroom windows had made the room pitch dark, he had locked the door before they'd drifted asleep and felt secure with Andy's naked body wrapped around him. With the absence of her warmth, panic bolted through his gut.

"Andy?" he called out to the quiet room, hoping she was merely using the bathroom. He waited a beat before grabbing his cell phone and illuminating the space around him. It was 7:10 in the morning.

The ensuite bathroom was empty.

Heart racing, he quickly changed back into the clothes Andy had torn off him before navigating through the maze of hallways and starting down the grand staircase to the main floor. He finally experienced a tick of relief when hearing Andy's light-hearted laughter before spotting her seated across from a slender blonde woman in the same spot Oswald and Trevor had brought them up-to-date the night before. Brock's stomach grumbled in appreciation of the aroma of something baking.

"Look who's finally up," Trevor grumbled as Brock's foot hit the bottom step. "Glad you're keeping a close eye on your woman, Resner."

Brock spotted the jealous prick alongside Oswald in the attached kitchen, working with various ingredients as a pan of something simmered on the stovetop.

"Now, Trevor," the blonde woman scolded in a faint British accent, "there's no need to be a wanker."

Laughing under his breath, Brock decided he already liked the woman who was presumably Andy's pseudo-mother. In a pale pink pants outfit suitable for a runway, she was striking with piercing dark brown eyes and sharp features that wouldn't go unnoticed in the largest of crowds. "You must be Emma," he said to her.

The woman's face lit with a wide smile. "And you must be the charming lad who's swept my hard-nosed Velora off her feet."

Behind her, Andy grunted. "I told you, it's *Andy*."

Emma rose onto her high heels with a tinkling

laugh and kissed each of Brock's cheeks. The elegant heels made her nearly as tall as him, and she gave off a pleasantly floral scent. "It's lovely to meet you, Brock."

"Likewise," he replied before lowering to settle in at Andy's side. "I was worried when I woke, and you were gone," he whispered into her ear. "Next time, leave a note."

"Sorry, babe," she whispered before brushing her lips across his unshaven jaw. "I promise I will."

"Guess it only took a mere wipe of your wits to find true love," Emma sang dreamily. "I suppose there's always a silver lining to the end of every tragic story."

"My 'story' is far from over," Andy told her sharply. "I assume the team has been assembled to find my father's killer and stop whoever's after the diamond."

"How do you propose we go about doing that?" Trevor asked from behind the kitchen island. "Pop over to Russia to take out Babanin and his entire army?"

Brock directed a sharp look in his direction. "Whether or not Babanin is over here or in Russia isn't our immediate concern. You all need to decide how to secure the diamond so the target is no longer on Andy's back. She can't keep running like this."

"He's right." Andy squeezed his leg affectionately. "What were we planning to do with it? Hand it over to the proper authorities?"

"It's essentially part of a treasure trove, love," Emma replied with a graceful shrug of her shoulders. "We're under no obligation to turn it over to anyone."

"Finders keepers," Trevor added.

Brock's stomach twisted with unease. If the diamond was actually up for grabs by whoever had found it, he was willing to bet it was valuable enough to make anyone in the room turn on the team. At that point in time, he didn't have a valid reason to trust any of them.

"Allow me a moment to play the devil's advocate," Emma added with some hesitation. "Are we absolutely *certain* it's Babanin behind all of this?"

Oswald lifted one eyebrow. "What're you suggesting? That it was someone from within the team?"

She mirrored his questioning expression. "It's certainly possible, is it not?"

An uneasy silence spread over the room.

Although Brock didn't speak up, he wholeheartedly agreed. As far as he was concerned, everyone who knew about the diamond could be a suspect. His suspicion grew as Trevor turned away, suddenly more interested in tending to whatever was inside the oven.

Frustration was written all over Andy's face as she gritted her teeth. "So what do we do about the diamond now? Sell it? Break it off into nine pieces?"

"No one's breakin' anything apart," a gruff voice announced.

They all turned to watch a stocky man with beady, dark eyes set close together enter the room. He wore a crumpled sports jacket with dark blue jeans, strawberry blond hair greased back with an excessive amount of product. The way he regarded everyone in the room with suspicion and shifty eyes, Brock wondered if the man was on something.

Trevor was the first to break the silence with a sharp laugh. "I'd say it's good to see you, Spence, but I don't think that's ever been the case."

"Who rang him?" Emma asked, folding her arms with a look of displeasure.

"I did," Oswald answered. "It's important we get the entire team's input before we make our next move."

"Where's the blue diamond?" Spence demanded, throwing everyone in the room a narrowed glare. "I ain't got all day for this."

Everyone in the room regarded Andy, waiting for her to answer.

"It's somewhere safe," Brock assured them.

"Who're you?" Spence snarled as he took on a threatening stance that made Brock shift uncomfortably.

"He's Velora's new beau," Emma answered. "It's a long, rather complicated story."

"Since when do we trust outsiders?" Spence asked.

"Since *Velora* suffered a head wound and needed an outsider's help," Brock replied, lifting his chin. "I've been protecting her, trying my best to keep her alive."

Spence's eyes darted over to Oswald. "Where're the others?"

Oswald removed the pan from the stovetop and turned to face Spence. "Grant's in Singapore on business, can't make it here for a few days. He said to FaceTime him once we're all here. Rich and Penny should roll in around noon. I have yet to hear anything from Gunnar."

"Gunnar's been off-grid the past few months," Trevor told him. "Good luck getting through to him."

Oswald grunted in reply before addressing everyone in the room. "There's biscuits and gravy up for grabs. Go ahead and help yourselves. We'll talk business after the Wrights arrive."

"Who died and put you in charge?" Spence sniggered.

"Jonesy made it clear since day one that Oswald would be his successor were anything to happen," Emma told him sharply, crossing her arms. "I don't imagine *you're* in any position to take charge. Need I remind you that you're still on probation for your last muck up?"

"I don't need some uppity British bitch tellin' me my business." Spence's gaze became dangerously dark as he made his way closer to her. "What're you gonna do now that Jonesy isn't around to warm your bed when you're stateside? Spread your legs for Oswald to justify your place on the team?"

"That's enough!" Oswald barked, stepping in between them to tug on Spence's arm. "Speak to her like that again, and you're out of here! Maybe even off the team. We clear?"

"*Crystal.*" Spence reclaimed his arm while casting Emma one last dangerous look. "I see where your loyalties lie. I see all of y'all and what you're doin'." Pulling a pack of cigarettes from his shirt pocket, he sulked back out the way he entered.

Emma shook her head and started for the kitchen, clearly unfazed by his outburst. As the others trailed behind, Andy and Brock stayed on the couch. "I definitely don't trust that guy," Andy whispered.

Brock glanced around the room, watching Oswald and Emma converse with matching frowns as they formed a line behind Trevor. "I don't know that anyone here does."

Andy's gaze darkened. "Do you suppose he could be the one who tried to steal the diamond… who shot my father?"

Shrugging, Brock squeezed her hand inside his. "I think anything's possible."

"But we have to trust someone. The two of us don't know enough to figure this out on our own. We need insider information."

As Oswald started for them, Brock whispered to her, "I think we can trust your father's old friend. Either he's an excellent actor or the guy's an open book and truly cares about you."

"You two not hungry?" Oswald asked, lifting his heaping plate of biscuits and gravy topped with two poached eggs. "I promise I'm not too terrible of a cook. Kept your daddy alive on the days he was too involved in hunting to feed himself."

"Actually, we're starving," Andy answered. Scraping her top teeth over her bottom lip, she eyed him with lingering skepticism. "But as soon as we're finished eating, there's something Brock and I want to show you."

Inside Andy's walk-in closet, Oswald scratched his head while gazing down at the tray filled with sparkling jewels. "Not sure what you're worried about, darlin'. I'm sure you were holdin' onto these... waitin' for the right time to sell them. I have a similar stash myself."

Andy's shoulders relaxed somewhat. "You don't think I was hiding them from the team?"

"Your daddy had this tray installed after the break-in. Not sure who else knew about it, but he told me."

"I'm guessing you've seen the blue diamond before?" Brock asked, surprised that Oswald had barely glanced at it since Andy had opened the compartment,

"Only once." He shrugged before giving Andy a tentative look. "May I?"

"Go ahead," she conceded with a bob of her head.

Oswald removed a handkerchief from his pocket and used it to pluck the blue diamond from the tray. He held the large jewel in the palm of his hand, eyes narrowed as he inspected it closer. "Hold on."

"What is it?" Andy asked, her voice tight.

Oswald snagged the pair of reading glasses from the pocket of his button-down shirt and slipped them over his nose. "I'll be damned," he grunted in a dryly amused sound. "I do believe this diamond may be more valuable than we originally thought."

Brock's throat tightened as he leaned over Oswald's shoulder. He didn't like the sound of that. Andy was already in enough danger. "Why would you say that?"

"There's a symbol etched into the side," Oswald responded thoughtfully. "It looks kinda like a set of waves. It's in the same style as the other symbols."

Andy and Brock exchanged a surprised look before she asked, "What other symbols?"

"They're written on a map your daddy had." Oswald lowered the diamond and released a pleased grin. "One that will lead us to an even bigger treasure."

CHAPTER 19

Andy

AS HER GAZE danced between her father's oldest friend and the rare diamond still resting in the palm of his hand, Andy's heart raced. "A *bigger* treasure?" she wheezed out. "How big are we talking?"

"Hundreds of millions. Maybe even more." Oswald gave a half-shrug like it didn't matter. For someone who seemed to get off on being flashy, he was unexpectedly casual about precious treasures. "At this point, we can't be sure of its total value."

Brock whistled as Andy blinked repeatedly while trying to comprehend what he was saying. "Who else knows it exists?"

"Your daddy only confided in you an' me." Oswald glanced at the closet's entrance before lowering his voice. "He'd discovered an old copy of a treasure map long before we recovered this diamond.

He thinks it was drawn up by Peg Leg Paulsgrave so he'd remember where he stashed the rest of O'Malley's treasure."

Andy felt a stab of unease. Had her father died trying to protect the map? "Maybe whoever's after me knows about the map," she commented. "Maybe that's why they killed my father, but let me go. They needed someone who could lead them to it."

She took the diamond from Oswald and slowly rotated it in her fingers until she spotted the faint etching. "I still had this after he was killed. It wouldn't have taken much to find it on me, but instead, I was left for dead. It would make sense if they had their eye on a bigger prize."

"Or maybe something had them spooked before they could get to you," Oswald decided.

"What's the story with that Spence guy?" Brock asked him. "Can he be trusted?"

"Jonesy seemed to think so." Eyes flickering up to the ceiling, Oswald scratched his head. "I personally never liked the guy, though. He spent ten years in the clink for grand larceny back in the eighties."

"That's enough to make him a suspect," Brock decided.

With a shake of his head, Oswald chuckled. "Except Spence is an idiot. He was caught because he tried to use a stolen credit card to book a flight to

Acapulco. I don't think he has the skillset required to round up a team of professional hitmen to come after our girl. Jonesy only added him to the team because he has valuable connections in the black market."

Andy tapped her lips thoughtfully. She'd been starting to believe the Russian mobster story until Emma had suggested there could've been a traitor amongst the team like she'd originally suspected. From what little she knew, she wasn't convinced she could trust a single team member she'd met thus far. But considering Oswald had known about the hidden compartment in her bedroom, she suspected her father had trusted his friend most of all. "What about the others who aren't here yet?"

"Rich and Penny, the team's archeologists, are humble folks...tend to keep to themselves. They have twice as much as the rest of us since there are two of them, but they continue to live in a quaint little two-bedroom in a Minneapolis suburb and drive rusted-out cars. They've passed most of their riches onto their adult children. I can't see them harmin' anyone considerin' they're perfectly content with what they have." He set the diamond back inside the tray with extra care, like it was a bomb about to discharge. "Grant's already a self-made millionaire but he's a greedy bastard who collects exquisite toys. Jonesy brought him on to fund our hunts. Based on what I know about him and his history of backstabbing his partners in the past to become more wealthy, I wouldn't check him off the list of our suspects just yet."

A hum vibrated against Brock's throat. "What about that Gunnar guy? Does he go off-grid often?"

"Half the time, we don't hear a peep from Gunnar when we reach out. Nothing unusual there. No one knows where he lives. He only attends the team meetings when he feels like it. Even then, he doesn't say much. He's former military, like Trevor and Vel—Andy, here. Guy seems overly suspicious of everyone. I think he saw some shit while serving that made him that way."

Brock sneered, appearing unimpressed. "How long has he been on the team?"

"Must be a decade or so by now. He's the last one Jonesy added before declaring we'd go by the 'Treasured Ten' moniker."

"Did my father really have a thing for Emma?" Andy wondered. "I mean, did they sleep together like Spence suggested?"

"They were lovers," Oswald confirmed with a slow smile. "Your daddy tried to convince her several times over the years to move in with him, but she had no interest in relocating here. She's completely harmless. It tore her up something awful when I rang her with the news about your daddy. She threw up, then sobbed like a newborn. I truly believe she loved him."

The possibility that her father was in love with someone unavailable tore her up inside. Had he ever known true happiness after her mother had left them? "That may be true, but I don't think we can rule anyone out yet."

"What about Trevor?" Brock intervened. "Do you trust him?"

"Hasn't given me any reason not to," Oswald said, eyes narrowed on Andy. "Don't you?"

She thought about it, shrugged. "It's too early to decide one way or another. I say for now, we don't tell anyone else about this map," she declared, locking the diamond and other treasures inside the hidden compartment.

"Well, now," Oswald protested, "If we want to decipher the symbols, we'll have to show it to Penny. She specializes in symbology—spent a solid three years traveling the world when she was younger, studying that kind of thing."

"I guess that'd be okay, but only if you're extremely confident we can trust her."

"We can. I'd bet my sixty-five Mustang on it."

"Fine. Where's the map?" she asked.

With a determined look, Oswald lifted his chin. "Somewhere safe."

"Now you don't trust *me*?" Andy huffed.

Darting a doleful look in Brock's direction, Oswald wrapped his fingers around her forearm. "Come with me, darlin'. I'd prefer to have a word with you alone."

Catching Brock's irritated stare cast in Oswald's direction as he slinked out of the closet, Andy rose on her tiptoes to dust his lips over his. "Relax. I won't let him take me far. If I'm not back in two minutes, you can come to my rescue."

"Until we know who we can trust, you need to be extra careful. Even if he claims to be your father's closest buddy, he could still be the enemy." His arms clamped around her, dragging her in for a deeper kiss. Andy briefly became lost in the brush of his lips, the sweep of his tongue. She longed for a life of normalcy in which she could focus on nothing other than her feelings for Brock and how her body responded to his touch.

Once she broke away to join Oswald inside her bedroom, she closed the door to the bathroom and tilted her head. "What's going on?"

Oswald began to pace the room. "I don't trust this new man of yours who seemingly came out of nowhere. You haven't shown any interest in being with a man in *years.*" He peered at her from the corner of the eye. "What's so special about this guy? Where'd you find him?"

"He caught me stealing from him, yet he still wanted to help when I thought I had nowhere else to go," she admitted among a long breath. "It's a complicated story—not as cut and dried as it sounds. Still, I have no reason to doubt his intentions. He's had several opportunities to steal the diamond. If that's what he was after, he could've split long ago. I trust him...he seems to truly care about protecting me." *And I think I might be in love with him,* she silently added with a smile playing on the corners of her lips.

Oswald's eyebrows lowered. "Or maybe he got insider information about the map, and he's using you. Wooing you so he can get close to the real treasure."

Eyes squeezed shut, she shook her head. There was *no way* that was Brock's intention. She refused to believe such a wild, unfounded theory could be true. She met Oswald's suspicious expression and forced a smile. "I appreciate what you're saying, but I think we should focus on the team. I've been shot several times but never wounded. Someone my father trusted might simply be trying to scare me into leading them to this map."

"Still think it could be Babanin." Oswald stopped

pacing and let out a low groan. "Can't imagine anyone your daddy trusted would be capable of killing him in cold blood like that."

"Greed can make people do unimaginable things," Andy muttered. "Listen, Oswald. Brock is the one who decided you could be trusted out of everyone else. You could extend an olive branch and return the gesture."

"Fine, but he's still going to have to prove himself to be noble."

Hours later, Andy and Brock waited for Oswald, leaning against the walls of what could only be described as a bunker. Thick concrete surrounded a table and chairs beneath a bare lightbulb hanging from a roughed-in opening in the ceiling. Andy was becoming stir-crazy in her father's fortified mansion. She could almost literally feel the walls closing in around them. A shutter ripped through her when she considered Oswald may have tricked them into their own imprisonment.

"It'll be okay," Brock told her, kissing the top of her head while pulling her close. "I have a good feeling about Oswald."

"I wish he could say the same about you," she

replied with a short laugh. "He's suspicious of your involvement with me."

"Can't blame him. I would be, too, if I were in his position."

Just then, Oswald strode into the room behind a short, robust woman in an outdated tracksuit and sneakers, bronze hair styled in a no-nonsense haircut. She looked sternly at Andy before pulling her in for a firm hug. "Dammit, kid. You had us scared half to death."

"Sorry," Andy simply replied, unwilling to rehash the details yet again.

"And you must be the new boyfriend," the woman said to Brock with a warm smile and a single eyebrow lift. "Our girl chose well."

"Brock," he said, offering his hand.

"Penny," she answered, giving his hand a firm shake.

Oswald held up a metal cylinder in one hand, and clamped his other hand on Penny's shoulder. "I asked you to come here alone because I wanted to show you something in strict confidence—no telling the rest of the team until we're certain there wasn't a breach of trust."

Penny bobbed her head. "Understood. Can't say I trust half of them anyway. I never understood why

Jonesy trusted so many strangers to know his secrets."

"He didn't," Oswald confirmed. "There was a pretty big one he'd only trusted with me and his daughter."

Everyone in the room seemed to collectively hold their breaths as Oswald unscrewed the top of the metal cylinder. He carefully removed a battered piece of thick paper and unrolled it across the table. It was torn and yellowed, covered in faded symbols and squiggly lines across a hand-drawn map.

"Where'd you find this?" Penny with among a breathy gasp.

"Jonesy discovered it around the same time he learned about the blue diamond."

She hunched over to slowly scan the map's contents. "Some of these are Celtic symbols. The rest are exactly what they appear—drawings of real-world items." She tapped her finger on one of the symbols. "Like that's clearly a cannon—the type they used in the seventeen hundreds. Cannon was a common name in Ireland. The original Gaelic form was O'Canain, which derived from the word 'cano.' It translates to 'wolf cub'."

Andy leaned in at her side. "The diamond symbol behind it…there are waves etched into the blue diamond. Do you suppose that's in reference to a beach? What if he meant the cannon symbol to be a literal translation?"

"Like *Cannon Beach,*" Brock agreed with excitement in his tone. "That drawing above it looks like the Haystack formation."

Andy recalled something her father had said to her in a recent dream.

"...sometimes art imitates life, baby girl. And sometimes there are truths to fiction."

A rush of excitement swept through her. Eyes wide, she met Brock's equally excited gaze across the table. "I think the treasure is hidden somewhere near Astoria."

CHAPTER 20

Brock

AFTER HOURS of hashing out the fine details of the map with Penny and narrowing it down to a specific cave, Brock and Andy prepared to return to Astoria. She quickly selected several outfits from both her closet and her father's, deemed suitable for trekking through caves, and stuffed them inside a small roller bag. Brock couldn't help but wonder what would happen after they recovered the treasure—if, in fact, it was still there. Would she want to stay in her father's home indefinitely? Would she agree to move in with him instead? He worried once she experienced the adrenaline of treasure hunting, she'd want to do it again. He couldn't stand the idea of her constantly being in extreme danger.

When he exited the ensuite bathroom, he found Trevor looming on the threshold of her bedroom with the expression of a sad puppy. "Can I have a minute alone with Andy?"

The fine hairs on the back of Brock's neck rose. It wasn't so much that he was jealous—he just didn't trust the guy. "If this is about your feelings for her—"

"I know about the map," he blurted. "Is that why she wanted to talk with Oswald alone? Did you find the rest of the treasure?"

Andy emerged from the bathroom behind Brock. "How did you know about the map?" she demanded, her voice sharp with anger. She started for him, appearing ready to grab him by the throat. "Are you the one who shot my father and left me for dead in the woods?"

Trevor's jaw hardened. *"No, dammit.* I would *never* do that to you."

"Who told you about the map?" Brock asked, ready to throttle the guy for upsetting her.

"Not that it's any of your business, but *she* told me," Trevor insisted. "Like I said, we were extremely close." With a regretful look, he regarded Andy. "We didn't have any secrets between us. At least not before."

"That may have been true, but you need to stop looking at me like a schoolboy with a crush," she scolded. "I'm not the same person you knew. My father's death changed me, for better or worse. Whatever we may've had before is over now." She slipped her arm around Brock's waist. "I'm not saying the two of us can't be friends again someday, but you have to accept that I'm with Brock now."

"Fine," Trevor grumbled, eyes darting to the floor. "But I want to help you recover the treasure."

Andy clicked her tongue and shook her head. "That's not going to happen. You haven't given us a valid reason to trust you."

"Let me go along, and I won't tell the others about it," Trevor threatened, his eyes darkening. "And I want a fair cut. I helped recover the blue diamond. Without it, you wouldn't have interpreted the map, right?"

"You want us to trust you as you're resorting to blackmail?" Andy snapped. "I fail to see how that works in your favor."

His eyes seemed to darken even more. "*Velora* wouldn't have pushed me into doing it. She would've let me in because she trusted me."

"*Velora* is no longer," she reminded him with a sneer. Then she paused and forced out a short breath. "Okay. I'll probably be a little rusty when it's time to maneuver through the caves. It'd be nice to have someone experienced along to help." She stabbed a finger through the air in his direction. "But if you try to double-cross us in any way—"

"I won't," he promised.

"We're leaving here in an hour, shortly after we talk to the others," Brock told him. "Better be ready, or we'll go without you."

Trevor tilted his head. "What exactly are you going to tell them?"

"That we're relocating to somewhere safe until we find the person who's put a hit out on me," Andy answered, her tone unusually authoritative. "Say anything that makes them suspicious, and you're out."

Trevor's lips quirked with a smart-assed smirk. "Sure thing."

As he slinked away, Brock's phone vibrated with a text. He slipped it out from his jeans pocket, finding a text from Rio.

The cave in question is only accessible during low tide. It'll be lowest at 1:27 a.m. Should I be concerned about your sudden interest in caving?

Andy glanced over his shoulder to read the text and let out a long sigh. "Looks like we have another long night ahead of us."

Brock merely kissed the top of her head in

response. He had a bad feeling about their plan but couldn't place what made him so uneasy. More than likely it was because there were still too many unknowns, and Andy's circle of trust was becoming too wide.

Once everyone gathered in the great room where Oswald informed the remaining team members they were leaving to find a more secure hideout for Andy, Spence aimed a murderous glare at Oswald.

"What about the diamond?" he snarled from his perch at the edge of the room. Brock noted the guy was never more than a handful of feet away from an exit. "You made us travel all this way, and we ain't even decided what we're gonna do with it!"

"It's in a secure location," Oswald promised. "This is like any other hunt, Spence. Jonesy would've held onto the treasure until it was time to move it."

"You're not Jonesy," Spence reminded him with a sneer.

Oswald tongued the toothpick inside his mouth and threw Spence a stern look. "No, I'm not. If you're worried I'll double-cross you, I can cut you a check right now for a quarter of your share." He glanced at Emma and the Wrights. "That goes for everyone."

Penny's husband, a tall and willowy man with a hallowed face and sharp features, pushed his tortoise-rimmed glasses up his nose. Brock could envision the archeologist standing behind a podium in a college classroom, especially as he wore the stereotypical dull brown sports jacket over a button-down and khakis. "That seems fair enough."

"Shut up, Dick!" Spence spat at him. "Your homely ass probably ain't got nothin' ridin' on this diamond! I have debts to pay—serious ones! The kind that'll get your throat slit for not repayin'!"

"Sounds like *your* problem," Trevor muttered under his breath as he shifted his bag from one shoulder to the other.

Spence redirected his anger at Trevor. "It's as fishy as hell that you're runnin' off with them. We all know you an' Velora had somethin' going on before she went missin'. How do we know the three of you ain't plannin' on double-crossing us all and runnin' away with the loot?"

"What *exactly* would you have us do?" Emma asked Spence. "Everyone in this room knows it'll take months to secure a proper buyer...maybe even years. And considering someone is willing to commit murder to get their hands on it, it's not safe to handle it out in the open. It's best to keep it hidden...at least for now."

"She's right," Grant Becker, the millionaire, agreed from the flatscreen TV across the room. They'd caught him while he was in New York, awaiting his final flight to Portland. The soft features on his round face and short black hair were mostly unremarkable, giving him an average appearance. Seeing him in the streets, Brock would've assumed he was a lawyer or a banker. "The sale isn't something we would want to rush anyway. I've contacted some of my connections and may have found an interested buyer. But he's currently tied up in other sizable acquisitions that require his full attention. I wouldn't count on him reaching out anytime soon."

With an audible huff, Spence stormed out of the room.

"We all know he'll get over it," Oswald told the team. "His displeasure is nothing new."

Grant's voice and image became distorted on the screen as he said, "The rest of us trust you to do the right thing, Oz."

"He's right," Emma concurred with a sharp nod. "We trust that this is the best decision for the team."

Both Wrights nodded along with her.

If Brock still hadn't suspected a traitor among them, he would've felt guilty for lying to them. He also wasn't entirely convinced they hadn't trusted the wrong person.

Minutes after the Wrights left, Oswald loaded their baggage into the back of his souped-up pickup truck with an extended passenger cab. Brock's discontent grew with every second that ticked past. Although Oswald had assured them Spence's vehicle was gone, Brock half expected an ambush by Spence and was eager to leave. The tension rolling off of the convict earlier had been palpable.

"What's taking Trevor so long?" Brock grumbled to no one in particular.

"I'll go check on him," Oswald volunteered, starting for the house.

He passed Emma on the way, whispering something to her before she approached Andy and Brock with a sad smile. She still looked regal in her pantsuit, but her eyes were shadowed with sadness and exhaustion. Her lips quivered as she brushed Andy's hair over her shoulder. "It seems I only had a moment with you while you were here, dear girl." She turned to Brock. "When will you bring her back to me?"

"That'll be up to her," Brock decided, meeting Andy's gaze. "This is her journey. She needs to proceed at her own pace."

Eyes flickering back and forth between Andy's,

Emma molded her hands around Andy's face. "You're certain you don't remember anything from before, love? Not a *thing* about what happened to your father or what you were doing in that forest?"

Brock suddenly wanted to pull Andy close, away from the strange woman's grip. From the tone of Emma's voice, it almost seemed as if she was worried Andy *did* remember something. He wondered if Andy thought the same as she subtly removed Emma's hands from her face.

"Nothing," Andy confirmed with an awkward smile slipping over her lips. "But I'm sure it'll return eventually."

They all spun around with the sound of Oswald yelling, "In the truck! Now!" His expression was filled with darkness as he raced back toward them. He made a grand sweep of his arm in Emma's direction. "You too, woman!"

"Why on earth would I do that?" she balked in a quivering voice.

"What's wrong?" Andy asked simultaneously.

"Don't waste time by asking foolish questions!" Oswald roared, opening the passenger's door and practically hoisting Emma inside.

Sensing something was seriously amiss, and they were in danger, Brock took Andy's arm and guided her inside the backseat, jumping in a second behind her. Brock and the two women braced themselves as Oswald tore out the driveway with gravel spitting out from beneath the tires.

"What's happening?" Andy asked, turning in her seat to glance out the back window. "Where's Trevor?"

Jaw clenched, Oswald eyed her through the rearview mirror. "Trevor's dead."

CHAPTER 21

Andy

ANDY'S STOMACH folded over itself, and her mind raced enough to make her dizzy. Just as the news of her father's death, she didn't know how to feel about Trevor's, but there was undoubtedly an added factor of immediate fear knowing someone had been murdered a handful of yards from where they'd stood. Although she'd been irritated when Trevor had threatened to tell the others about the map, she wouldn't have wished him *to die* because of it.

"What do you mean Trevor's *dead?*" she demanded. "How is that possible? We just saw him like twenty minutes ago!"

"Blimey!" Emma gasped, slapping a hand over her lips. "Are you quite sure?"

Oswald scanned every direction as he gunned the

truck through the dense woods. "I found him in the half bath near the entrance…throat slit. There was no saving him. He'd lost too much blood."

Brock's hand slid over Andy's as he snarled at Oswald. "Why the hell did we just leave? Did you at least call an ambulance?"

"Did you want to stick around and see if they'd come after Andy next?" Oswald snarled back.

A trickling unease made its way down Andy's back. "How do we know *you* didn't kill him?" she near-whispered.

"She's right," Brock said, gripping Andy's hand. "Pull over."

Oswald grunted with disapproval. "I'm not pulling over until we're far from the house and certain we aren't being followed."

When Andy passed Brock an uneasy glance, he clenched his fingers more tightly around hers.

Before long, Andy and Brock fell asleep in the back of Oswald's truck. They didn't wake until Oswald pulled up outside Astoria's city limits in front of a truck stop with dozens of diesel pumps and signs advertising showers and long-term parking spaces. Although darkness had fallen during their road trip, the parking lot surrounding a 24-hour diner was well-lit and occupied by half a dozen rigs.

"What's the plan now?" Oswald asked, glancing at each of them through the rearview mirror.

"Have you heard anything from the rest of the team?" Andy asked, pulling away from Brock's embrace while rubbing the sleep from her eyes. "Was anyone else hurt?"

Oswald grunted, clearly not pleased. "They all split once they discovered Trevor's body. No one wanted to be implicated in his murder. The Wrights called the murder in anonymously from a public phone."

Andy's eyes fluttered shut for a moment. Would she feel more empathy for Trevor once her memories returned? He had clearly been a loyal friend—she only wished it hadn't taken his death to prove it once and for all. It also seemed more plausible than before that someone from the team had killed him. A traitor walked among them.

"Brock and I will find our own way from here," she told Oswald, briefly glancing Emma's way. She didn't trust either of them enough to give them Brock's address and knew Skye would jump at her request for a ride. "Keep your phones handy—we'll keep you updated as soon as possible. I doubt we'll get a signal in the caves, so it could be a while."

"You're still going through with the plan?" Emma inquired, her voice tight with concern. "I think it would best if you lie low until the danger dissipates, love."

"I'm tired of hiding and running," Andy told her with a firm shake of her head. "It's time to finish this once and for all." There were still so many unanswered questions about her past, and she wasn't exactly confident she could maneuver her way through the cave, but she all at once felt in charge of the situation. She wanted to think it was something she had inherited from her father. "Brock has a friend in the local law enforcement. Before we head to the caves, we'll tell him exactly who he needs to look for tomorrow morning in case you cross us and we go missing."

"I assure you that won't happen," Emma snipped, sounding slightly offended. "We care for you deeply, sweet girl. Should anything happen to you..." Her voice tightened with a small sob.

Remembering what Oswald said about Emma's reaction to her father's death, Andy felt a slight pang of empathy for the woman. Still, she acknowledged it could simply be an act for Andy's benefit.

"She's right," Oswald agreed. "We're here for you, kiddo. We want to see this through just as much as you do. If you need anything, we won't be far away."

Brock gave Andy's thigh a reassuring squeeze. "Whether or not you're telling the truth, I can assure you nothing bad will happen to her as long as I'm around."

Moments later, they'd retrieved their luggage from the back of the truck. As Oswald's headlights pulled away, Brock called his sister while Andy paced the parking lot. It felt as if there wasn't anyone left on the team they could trust. They needed a fail-proof plan for what to do with the treasure if it was truly where they expected to find it. She hoped Brock's old friend from the Coast Guard would be willing to give them a lift—one last time.

While Brock was wrapping up the call to his sister, headlights veered in their direction. Andy gripped Brock's bicep to get his attention. They both stiffened when the red and blue lights blipped on top of the police cruiser. *The gig is up*, Andy thought. They'd come to arrest her for all she'd done.

"Skye?" Brock grumbled into his phone. "Stay put for now. I'll call you right back."

As Brock slipped his phone into his pocket, the passenger's window on the cruiser slid down. From the driver's seat, Knox's lips twisted with a condescending smile. "How was *Portland*?"

"What are you doing here?" Brock asked, stepping in to shield Andy from his friend. Andy found it enduring that he still possessed an innate instinct to protect her even after they'd discovered she was a highly trained soldier.

"The gig's up, old friend," Knox stated. "You two are up to something, and I'd bet my badge it has something to do with that dead treasure hunter they found by Cave Junction."

Brock barked out a short laugh. "Not this again. Knox, *buddy*, you're being paranoid."

One of Knox's eyebrows lifted. "Then explain why you're standing out here in the dark with luggage and no vehicle."

Sighing, Andy gripped Brock's elbow and whispered, "You trust him?"

"With my life," Brock confirmed quietly.

The tension in Andy's shoulders slowly began to deflate. They'd discussed the idea of clueing Knox into the situation as added backup, and she was starting to think it was the right thing to do. "We could use some coffee and a hot meal," she told Knox, motioning to the diner. "We'll tell you everything once we're inside."

Once Knox had a few minutes to digest their story, he leaned back to study Andy's terse expression. "You really don't remember a single thing before finding your old man dead?"

Andy shoved her half-consumed burger and fries away from her, unable to stomach any more. She wasn't exactly thrilled by the idea of running through a cave in the middle of the night, knowing they had a limited window of time to get the job done before the tide returned. "I've had flashbacks of conversations with my father from when I was little, and I experienced a few glimmers of familiarity here and there while visiting his home, but not much beyond that. According to the internet, my condition could last for *years*."

Brock draped an arm around her and dropped a kiss on her temple. "I did a little research of my own, and I think a good therapist might be able to help your memories return sooner. We'll find you someone once this mess is resolved."

Appreciation swelled inside Andy's belly. She'd give anything to accelerate the process, and she was pleased to hear Brock still planned to stay by her side despite the nightmare of a situation she'd dragged him into.

"I'm going into that cave with you," Knox announced, his tone firm. "I have all the gear you'll need. Besides, it's dangerous for a couple of amateurs to explore those caves alone at night. You could easily get lost or injured. People *die* from caving all the time—even those with years of experience."

"You've never mentioned you were into that kind of thing," Brock commented.

Knox lifted one shoulder. "One of my old girlfriends got me into it a few years back. I first agreed to it only because she looked hot in that gear. But it turned out to be pretty fun."

"According to my team," Andy reminded them, "I've been in caves countless times. I don't think I qualify as an amateur."

Eyebrows quirked, Knox chuckled. "Are you saying you don't remember your name, but you remember how to use ascenders and carabiners?"

She briefly closed her eyes and sighed. He had a valid point. She didn't even know what those terms meant. "Fine. But I don't know how the team will feel about a stranger tagging along. And I don't have the authority to bring you in on the proceeds from whatever treasure we find in there."

Knox hooked a thumb in Brock's direction. "Is this clown being paid to accompany you?"

Andy turned to meet Brock's warm gaze. "Not officially, but if he sticks around, I'm sure he'll reap the benefits."

Brock's lips bent with amusement. "I can promise I'm not interested in whatever wealth you come into. I'm more interested in the other benefits I'd get if you moved in with me."

Knox rolled his eyes. "And you can consider my presence a civil courtesy as an officer of the law." He leaned closer to Andy and gave a conspiratorial wink while lowering his voice. "Maybe you can also convince Brock to give me free growlers for the remainder of our lives."

"I think he's right," Brock said to Andy. "We have no business doing this without the help of someone experienced."

Andy only half-heartedly agreed.

It took an hour to pack the necessary gear once they arrived at Knox's place and another hour to drive to Canon Beach after Knox had stopped to fill his gas tank. Once they strapped into the equipment and entered the cave's opening, they were right on time. The tide had receded enough that they could easily navigate through the congested passageways. Knox led the way, slipping through cracks and crawling through caverns with the skill of a ninja. Andy had no problems keeping up with him, and Brock stayed close on her heels.

Just as she was beginning to feel confident about their adventure, they reached a tall cliff that descended into darkness, even beneath the triple beams of their headlamps. They each stood with their toes on the edge, assessing the drop.

"This is the fun part," Knox told them as he started tying knots in the cords and attaching them to each of their harnesses.

Sensing Andy's unease, Brock distracted her with a heated kiss that curled her toes and made her heart race. He then backed away with a teasing grin set against his lips. "Remember, you were trained as an Army Ranger. I'm sure you've faced far worse things. This'll be a piece of cake."

A heavy dampness clung to the air as they simultaneously lowered past the massive rocks illuminated by their headlamps. Adrenaline grew inside Andy with every foot they descended. The cavern was eerily quiet aside from water dripping in the distance and the occasional rustle of something nearby. She sensed the presence of creatures—specifically *bats*—among them and half expected the nocturnal beasts to swarm into her face at any moment.

The moment their feet landed on the rocky terrain

below, her lingering fear dissipated with the wheeze of her sharp breath.

Floating in a pool of crystal blue water among the massive rock walls was something she never thought she'd see in her lifetime.

"Oh, my God," she wheezed past a tight breath.

It was an honest-to-god pirate ship.

CHAPTER 22

Andy

ANDY SLAPPED a hand over her parted lips as her brain tried to register the grand sight looming before them. The pirate ship stretched a dozen stories into the humid air, stopping just feet beneath the cave's rocky ceiling. Decayed sails sagged from half a dozen masts, and gaping holes speckled the ancient wooden hull. A set of rusted canons erected at the ship's stern, still ready for battle. An equally rusted anchor the size of a compact car rested on the rocks below.

The ship was both beautiful and eerie to behold. How had it entered the caves? How long had it been stuck there? What happened to its crew? Had it belonged to Peg Leg Paulsgrave, or was it yet another thing he had stolen?

As a foul odor breached the air around them,

Andy doubted it could be the lingering scent of human decay, considering the ship had likely been there for *centuries*. Still, the rancid stench made her think of death.

"Wasn't expecting to see that," Brock commented at her side, his voice mixed with the same level of awe and disbelief. "Do you think we're the first ones to find it?"

"Let's go check it out," Knox suggested, moving forward.

Andy felt a nagging apprehension as they trailed after him. Knox seemed unfazed by the discovery of the incredible vessel. Was he too enamored by the notion of finding an invaluable treasure?

"If we find a large treasure inside that ship, how do we haul it out of here?" she asked Brock, keeping her voice low.

"I'm sure Oswald and the rest of your crew will know what to do," Brock whispered in her ear.

Unease slithered through Andy's stomach. Why was he whispering? Did he also sense there was something off about his friend?

At the edge of the water, Knox striped out of his gear and piled it on the rocks. Once he was down to his t-shirt and pants, he dove in. A moment later, he came to the surface. "Damn, that's cold!" He howled with a grin and waved, encouraging them to join him. "Come on!"

As Brock began to shed his gear, Andy pulled on his arm. "I think we made a mistake by bringing him into this."

"Knox is harmless," Brock insisted as he unhooked her harness. "Look at him! He's like a kid in a candy shop."

Deciding it was too late to turn back, Andy finished setting her gear into a pile by the others before diving into the water at Brock's side. The frigid chill wrapped around her bones, stealing her breath. She resurfaced in time to hear Brock yelling about the temperature.

"Suck it up," she called to him, rolling her eyes as she swam past.

Her muscles quickly adjusted to the chilling water, giving her an advantage over Brock. By the time she neared Knox and the crude rope ladder hanging over the ship, Brock was still several yards behind. He appeared exhausted as he stroked an arm along the surface on his right side.

"Kick faster!" she yelled in encouragement. "You're almost there!"

While she waited for him to catch up, Knox easily scaled the ladder. She watched intently as he hoisted himself over the deck railing and disappeared from sight. She couldn't shake the feeling that something wasn't right.

When Brock finally caught up, Andy insisted he climb the ladder ahead of her. Concerned by the paleness of his skin, she wanted to keep a close eye on him. She laughed under her breath when she realized the man she was falling for was a mere civilian, and she had presumably been through more taxing situations in training.

Brock waited for her at the top with water dripping down his face and the dismayed expression of someone who had nearly drowned. She allowed him to take her hand and assist her into the hull even though it wasn't necessary.

Not surprisingly, the main deck was riddled with holes, revealing portions of the deck below.

It was also littered with skeletal remains.

With each deep, steady breath Andy took, trying to ward off the cold seeping into her skin, the ship's staleness became more and more stifling. When her eyes swept across the various piles of bones, she noted they'd been scattered around. Without sorting through them and finding entire bodies, there was no telling how many pirates had perished on the ship.

"Looks like they were attacked," Brock muttered.

Andy scanned the entire ship's surface. "Where'd Knox go?"

Brock tipped his chin at a set of rickety stairs in the center of the ship's remains. "I'd guess below deck."

Together, they inched toward the stairway, taking each step with deliberate care. Andy winced each time the planks groaned beneath her wet feet. She paused at the top of the dark opening that descended into the belly of the ship. The soft glow of a candle breached the darkness as she called for Knox. Her voice was met with silence.

She glanced at Brock over her shoulder. "I don't like this. Something's off."

Brock's lips chattered when he said, "What do you want to do about it? Go back?"

A sparkling gleam of something ahead caught her eye as she contemplated her answer. She took three strides to discover an ornate wooden chest decorated in gold filagree and leather straps. It was like something out of the movies, overflowing with gold doubloons and rare gems, some mounted on rings or strung on necklaces. Despite thick layers of dust over the treasure, the genuine shine of the jewels was unmistakable.

Brock stepped in at her side and bent to blow some of the dust away from the top of the chest before he let out a sharp whistle. "Andy…this is…"

"I know," she whispered, bending to pluck one of

the doubloons from the chest. He bent over to study the treasure as she flipped it between her fingers and thumb. Printed on one side was the silhouette of what she guessed to be some kind of royalty surrounded by something in Spanish and the year 1798. It was considerably heavy in her grip.

Beside her, Brock bent to retrieve a necklace adorned with large rubies. Several large stones and doubloons spilled to the ground with its displaced weight. "A trove like this must be worth hundreds of millions—maybe more. To think it's been sitting here all this time, just waiting to be discovered."

A hot breath spread across the back of her neck. "You were right about one thing, Resner," Knox mused. "Even though her memory was gone, she would eventually come around. I knew she'd lead us to the loot that would set us up for life."

Andy jerked her head in Brock's direction, locking her shocked gaze with his.

Did he know his friend was crooked?

Had the man she was falling for been playing her all along?

But how? She'd sought *him* out at his brewery.

"How *could* you?" she demanded, rushing at Brock and pounding her fists against his chest. "I trusted you! I thought I was beginning to fall *in love* with you!"

With a shake of his head, Brock attempted to stop her fists. "Andy, I didn't—"

A metallic *click* sounded next to her ear. "He didn't betray anyone," Knox sneered. "*You* did."

With a jarring *whoosh* radiating through her skull, Andy's memories flooded back.

CHAPTER 23

Velora

THE MORNING of David Jones's death started like any other day since Velora had been honorably discharged from the Army nearly a decade prior. While she researched the details of their next hunt from the kitchen island, a cup of coffee clutched in one hand, her father and Oswald argued over the details of her father's latest fairytale in the next room.

"You're telling me Peg Leg Paulsgrave stole more than the blue diamond? How could he have escaped without O'Malley or his men noticing? You've always said he escaped in a row boat, Jonesy. Anything too heavy, and that rowboat would've sunk."

"I'm telling you, there's *much* more!" Velora's father disagreed. "Maybe the method by which he escaped was wrong. Or...or...maybe he really didn't die when he fell in the caves. Maybe he lived and went back for the rest of the treasure. Maybe he stole the entire *ship*."

"They found his wooden leg smashed to bits," Velora called out from the kitchen. "If legends are right, no one could've survived that fall."

"Stay out of this, Winona!" her father hollered back.

Oswald met Velora's wounded expression. "That's your daughter, *Velora*," he scolded his old friend. "Winona walked out on you when Velora was little. Remember?"

Velora's heart ached as her handsome father rubbed a trembling hand across his forehead. "Of course I remember! That's not something a man forgets!"

Although he still looked relatively young and fit for a man his age, his memory had been declining for the better part of a year. It was disheartening to realize he was developing dementia under the age of 60. Oswald refused to believe Velora whenever she broached the subject. *"The man has been through a lot in one lifetime,"* Oswald often said. *"And we're getting old. It's just a part of life. I forget things all the time."*

Silence settled over the room before the cloud lifted from her father's eyes. "I found a map," he half-whispered to his friend. "A treasure map. I think it was drawn up by Peg Let Paulsgrave."

Oswald gave a skeptical frown. "When? Where is it? Why didn't you mention this before?"

Her father glanced between his daughter and friend. "It's somewhere safe."

"Why don't you come get something to eat, Daddy?" Velora suggested, eyes cast downward. "I'll make you something if you'd like."

"That sounds like a splendid idea," Oswald pipped in, patting his friend's back. "Let's eat, Jonesy, and you can show me this map after our bellies are full."

Her father started for the bunker's entrance. "I'll go get the map so we don't waste any time." He scurried off, eyes lit with excitement.

"I'll keep an eye on him," Oswald volunteered, starting after his friend. He turned to her and added, "You know, just in case."

Velora's heart plummeted once they were both out of sight. In addition to her father's memory slipping, a growing part of her worried he was going insane. His belief in folklore had always been a little out there, but he had become more paranoid with time. He'd started creating a conspiracy theory on every hunt they made. He had helped them discover the blue diamond and insisted they leave it be until a feasible plan was in motion. His theory was if no one had found it after all this time, it would be best for it to stay right where it was—especially with Vladimir Babanin lurking around the area.

At least she knew the Russian billionaire wasn't merely a product of her father's imagination. They'd had several run-ins over the past year. He'd even once accosted her about the Treasured Ten when she'd made the mistake of going into town without the usual disguise.

"If you keep me informed of your every move when you hunt for the blue diamond," he'd said to her, his dark gaze and thick accent both tinged with unspoken dangers, *"I will make you wealthy beyond your wildest dreams. The others on your team would never have to know. It would be our little secret."*

Moments after she was left alone by her father and his friend, Gunnar strolled into the kitchen. He casually swiped her cup of coffee from her grip and took a long sip. "Good morning, beautiful."

Scoffing, she snagged the mug back. "Look what the cat dragged in. Seriously, it's been…what? Like 3 weeks? A month?"

He glared at her mug and started hacking. "That tastes like shit!"

"In Ranger training, we learned to drink it dark and black. I know you Marine pansies are used to sipping on Cappuccinos topped with whipped cream in the shape of a heart."

"Such a comedian," he quipped with a roll of his eyes. "Can I talk to you for a minute?" His gaze swept over the empty room. "Somewhere private?"

Velora's heart gave an extra thump when she nodded and silently trailed behind him to the grand stairway. When he disappeared into her bedroom, she glanced over her shoulder to check if they were being followed. A squeak stuck in her throat when she was unceremoniously yanked through the threshold.

Gunnar's eyes darkened as he looked down on her. "God, I've missed you."

Drawing her into his arms, they fell back against her door, slamming it shut. Velora allowed his lips to ravage hers for a full minute before she drew back, breathless. Despite their colored past and all the reasons they shouldn't be together, she had to admit the guy was one helluva a kisser. "I thought we decided we're done messing around like this."

With a hum, he feathered his lips across her neck. "Why? Saving yourself for Trevor?"

"It's not that, and you know it," she seethed. Trevor had declared his love for her countless times over the years, but she didn't feel anything for him beyond a deep friendship. Since the first day she met

Trevor in Ranger school, she had considered him a brother.

She nudged Gunnar back a step. "If anyone finds out—"

"What? Your old man will kick me off the team?" Releasing a snort deep inside his throat, he began to unbutton her blouse. "We agreed that doesn't matter anymore, remember?"

Once her shirt was open, revealing her bra, he bent to feather his lips across her chest. As badly as she wanted to push him away, she'd missed his touch while he'd been gone. She'd never admit it out loud, but she missed *him*.

Her fingers twisted through his hair as he began working on unzipping her trousers. "Where have you been? Or should I say, who have you been with this time?"

He grinned at her, his eyes lit with mischief. "You're the only girl for me, Lora. You know that."

"As if." She finally mustered the courage to shove him away. No matter how he made her feel, he was a womanizer. Plain and simple. She deserved better. She moved away to re-button her blouse. "I think my father's delusions are getting out of control to the point we need to do something. This morning, he was spewing nonsense about a bigger treasure left by Peg Leg Paulsgrave."

"You don't say," he replied with a thoughtful expression. "Maybe it's time to recover the blue diamond and move it somewhere safe."

Unease niggled Velora's brain. Other than her father, she and Trevor were the only two who knew of the diamond's precise location. If her father was of a sound mind, he wouldn't want her letting anyone else in on the secret.

Velora led the way through the cave with the agility of a jungle cat. Gunnar became her shadow, mimicking her every move. They recovered the precious jewel in less than two hours from the start.

Gunnar gave a low whistle once it was in the palm of Velora's hand. "I knew it was massive, but seeing it in person takes a person's breath away."

Velora tucked it underneath the tight strap of her sports bra. "It isn't worth anything until we find a buyer," she reminded him.

At the cave entrance, they found her father waiting in the dark. He wore a stern expression as he folded his arms over his chest.

Velora gasped. "Daddy, what—"

"I've watched you sidlin' up to my girl, gettin'

real friendly-like," her father growled, taking a step closer to Gunnar. "I knew you were up to no good."

"The diamond isn't safe here," Gunnar replied, lifting his chin defiantly. "We're doing this for the good of the team."

"The good of the team?" her father spat. His eyes narrowed. "Is that why you bought a one-way ticket to Moscow?"

Velora twisted away from Gunnar to face him head-on. "Is it true?"

Gunnar produced a pistol gripped in his right hand. "Hand the diamond over, Velora." He lifted it to her father's temple. "It's nothing personal."

Velora gritted her teeth, ready to fight for her father's life. "How can you say that? What happened to you? Why are you doing this?"

"I've been given a much better deal than any of you could ever offer."

"Don't give it to him, darlin'," her father pleaded, his expression as lucid as she'd seen in weeks. "He won't hurt me. We all know it. We're family."

Velora narrowed her eyes. "Babanin got to you. That's why you were planning to escape to Moscow. It's the only way you'd turn your back on us."

With a chuckle, Gunnar scratched his head with his free hand. "You always were the brains of this organization."

"I never should've trusted you," Velora's father snarled. "The minute I realized you were a dirty cop, I knew I'd made a mistake when I listened to Velora and brought you on." He struck out at Gunnar in an attempt to unarm him.

The gun fired.

As her father collapsed to the ground, Velora screamed and lunged at Gunnar. They wrestled for several minutes before she managed to recover the pistol. Gunnar recovered from the tumble and charged at her with a guttural roar.

She fired.

Despite having qualified as an expert marksman in the military, she missed her friend by a handful of inches. She wasn't shooting to kill—at least not yet. Realizing this, Gunnar squared his feet and stared at her.

"Come to Russia with me," he offered, extending a hand between them. "We'll go on treasure hunts of our own. Bahamian will make us rich beyond our wildest dreams."

"The next time I take a shot, I'm sinking a bullet into your skull. Don't make me do it, Gunnar."

He lingered for a moment before scurrying off into the dark. Shame for trusting him nearly made Velora crumple to the ground.

Once she was convinced he wasn't coming back,

she tucked the pistol into her pants and assessed her father's injury. She could still find a pulse when she pressed her fingers against his neck, but it was fragile. He was unconscious and didn't make a sound when she rolled him to his side. The bullet entered through his abdomen but didn't come back out through the other side.

She retrieved her phone from her pocket and wasn't surprised to discover the battery had died. She held the side buttons in, hoping for enough juice to summon the emergency feature, but the screen stayed dark. No one was coming to save them.

She lifted her father's limp body over her shoulders in a fireman's carry and started for the parking lot. Gunnar had left with the truck they'd brought, and the rest of the lot was empty. It would be a long hike back to civilization. But she could handle it.

Blowing out a breath of confidence, she started for the dense gathering of trees.

Darkness swallowed the forest as Velora trudged ahead, slicing through her path with the narrow light from her dying headlamp. Her teeth chattered on their own will from the damp cold clinging to the air. Every part of her ached from carrying her father for what she guessed to be several hours by the way the moon had shifted in the sky.

She was still a good 3 miles from the main road when the toe of her boot hooked on a thick tree root. Both her father and Velora went sailing through the air. She landed with something sharp digging into the back of her head.

"Velora?" came her father's groggy voice. She heard him dragging himself through the dirt before he appeared inside the headlamp's light. His eyes were filled with unshed tears. "Darlin', can you hear me?"

"Daddy," she whispered past the blinding pain encompassing her skull. "I'm gonna get you out of here." She paused, swallowing the massive lump building in her throat. Although she sensed this wasn't anything they would survive, she told him, "Everything's going to be okay."

"Afraid I'm not going to make it that far," he wheezed, glancing down at his blood-soaked jacket. His rough hands cradled her face as he offered a sorrowful smile. "I love you more than any treasure, my Velora. Don't you ever forget that, darlin'."

Dark spots danced through the headlamp's ray of light moments before Velora became lost in the darkness.

CHAPTER 24

Brock

BROCK'S STOMACH plummeted as his oldest "buddy" held a gun to Andy's head. How could he have been so wrong about Knox? Until this moment, he would've trusted him with his life. Instead, he may have placed Andy's life into the hands of a killer.

"I don't understand," Brock said to him. "What are you saying?"

"She once claimed she loved *me*." Darkness spread over Knox's gaze. "You have no idea how hard it was to watch her all this time…to witness the two of you forming a connection."

"You're joking," Brock blurted with an awkward laugh. However, based on his old friend's angry expression, he assumed it had to be true. "Wait, you're serious? When was this?"

"I had to keep an eye on her," Knox continued, ignoring Brock's question. "I figured she was lying about not remembering anything. I knew she'd eventually lead me to the treasure."

Brock studied Andy's expression as he absorbed Knox's revelation. Rather than appearing confused, she seemed calm and unaffected. Even if she didn't remember her past, why didn't she seem equally as baffled?

Something didn't feel right. As far as Brock knew, Knox had never been in love. "She's one of the women you saw while spending time in Cave Junction?" Brock guessed.

Knox's lips peeled back with a sneer. "It's more complicated than that."

"Put that down so we can talk about this," Brock suggested, gesturing to the gun. "What's killing her going to do? What are you hoping to accomplish?"

"She brought me to the treasure," Knox answered nonchalantly. "I don't need her anymore."

"He's the tenth member of the Treasured Ten," Andy said, her voice exceptionally steady considering her position. "Think about it, Brock. He's former military. And the day I first walked into your office, he'd insisted he knew me from somewhere. He's been watching me ever since I left the forest, hoping to get his hands on the diamond and the map together." She ground her teeth together. "He's the one who murdered my father. He planned to steal the blue diamond for Babanin."

Knox shrugged. "To be fair, I didn't shoot to kill."

"That's because you've always had shitty aim, even for a jarhead," she taunted. Her eyes sharpened on him. "He trusted you, Gunnar."

His lips parted with a sneer. "So you *do* remember me."

"Not until just now," she admitted, lifting her chin.

Brock drew in a sharp breath. "You remember? *Everything*?"

"Everything," she confirmed, eyes narrowed on Knox. "Must've been self-preservation so I'd forget my mistake of being with you."

Knox's expression darkened. The gun discharged, and Andy dropped to the ground.

"Andy!" Brock howled before launching himself at Knox.

More gunshots pierced the air, the sound higher and in more rapid succession than the first.

Someone else was shooting at them.

Brock dove to the ground, shielding Andy from further harm, while Knox crouched behind the chest. Glancing down at Andy, Brock sighed with relief when he saw the bullet had merely nicked the fleshy part of her shoulder. He slipped a hand along her jawline. "Andy, babe, stay with me."

"I'm fine," she groaned, eyes fluttering beneath their lids before they popped open. "Get off me. I need to bring that son-of-a-bitch down before he kills someone again."

"Put your weapon down!" Oswald demanded from somewhere in the darkness. "Don't make me do this, Gunnar! It doesn't have to end this way!"

Knox chucked in reply. "The only way this'll end is with me riding off into the sunset with this treasure, old man. Put *your* weapon down before I'm forced to take Andy as my hostage."

"You'll have to go through me to get to her," Brock snarled, hooking an arm around her waist. "I trusted you, Knox. You're like a brother to me!"

Knox glanced at him from behind his hiding spot. "This has nothing to do with you, Resner."

"The hell it doesn't! You shot the woman I love!"

Footsteps groaned from the deck above their heads. "I brought the state police along with me, Gunnar," Oswald announced from somewhere closer. "If you don't come out of there with empty hands in the next five seconds, I'll have no other choice but to take you out."

"I have better aim than you," Knox taunted.

From the corner of his eye, Brock spotted Knox

slipping away from them in the darkness. Andy shoved him aside. In the blink of an eye, she was back on her feet. "Stay behind me," she whispered before advancing into the darkness.

Brock mimicked the way she hunched down as she moved forward. They didn't make it far before they met up with Oswald, who handed Andy a pistol.

"You alright?" Oswald asked in the quietest of whispers.

"He just nicked me," she answered while checking the pistol for ammo.

"Where'd he go?" he asked.

"Unless there's more than one way out of here, he's still down here somewhere," she replied. "I doubt he's willing to part ways with the treasure."

"I was bluffin' about the state police, but Emma's upstairs, armed and waiting. She's a pretty damn good shot, too."

"What made you decide to come here?" Brock whispered.

"Emma spotted Gunnar in a police cruiser after we dropped you at the truck stop. We followed him with the intention of confrontin' him about not coming to the last meeting. After watching him interact with the two of you, we knew something was amiss."

"Good call." Andy patted his shoulder once. "Cover the stern; we'll head for the bow."

Brock exchanged a firm nod with Oswald before they scattered in opposite directions. The presence of more skeletons along their path wasn't as jarring as the idea of Knox hiding somewhere, willing to shoot anyone who got in his way.

The dusty air around them became suffocating as they crept through the old ship. Brock wasn't keen how the back of his neck tingled, but he kept up with Andy, admiring the way she forged ahead with complete confidence.

It seemed they were running out of ship once they saw a bit of light spilling through the broken deck above. Brock heard what he thought was a ragged breath. He turned his head in the direction of the noise before a gunshot blasted behind him.

"Andy!" He sprang forward to pull her down, but his foot caught on a wayward nail, and he fell.

Shots whizzed over his head from different directions, and wood from various parts of the ship exploded from stray bullets. A loud, manly grunt rang out before the firing ceased.

"I got him," Andy said as she helped Brock stand. "I'm not sure *where* I hit him, but he's on the move—I think he's headed toward the stairway. Try to keep up."

Grunting under his breath, Brock hurried after her as his action-hero of a girlfriend sprinted toward the stairs. Once the light from the cave spilled over the stairway, he noted the splotches of blood trailing up ahead.

"Look like you got him good," he commented.

"If he's still moving, it's not good enough," she called over her shoulder. "I'm not letting him get away a second time."

"Stop!" Emma cried out, drawing their attention to the aft side of the ship.

Andy and Emma simultaneously fired as Knox leaped over the side. They rushed to the spot where he'd been standing in time to catch the circular splash of water. The trio collectively held their breaths, waiting for him to resurface. By the time Oswald joined them, he still hadn't breached the water.

"He was injured," Emma reported. "Perhaps he's dead."

Eyes still trained on the water, Andy shook her head. "I doubt we could be that lucky."

"What do we do now?" Brock asked.

"This is where the fun begins, son," Oswald said. He tucked Emma against his side before he slapped Brock back with a merry laugh. "We get to extract the treasure and live like royalty."

Brock gathered Andy inside his arms and gave her a comforting kiss. He didn't care about the treasure, not really. He was already set for life, and Andy would be, too. He was merely relieved they had all survived his old friend's deviation.

Epilogue

Andy
8 months later

THE CRYSTAL clear blue water splashing against the yacht sparkled in the afternoon sunlight like a million diamonds. Behind them, colorful buildings and palm trees dotted the coastline beneath gentle mountains. Ahead, the French Rivera offered endless miles of peaceful adventures. With a contented sigh, Andy stretched her legs out on the canvas suspended above the open water rushing below and tilted her head back into Brock's lap, soaking in the intense sun's rays.

"This is the life," she declared with a sigh.

Grunting in agreement, Brock ran his fingers through her wild blond curls. "Who would've dreamed we'd have the means to retire at such a young age?"

"You already did," she mused. "And until you sell the breweries, you're technically still employed." She stroked her swollen belly. "But we won't feel this carefree in a few weeks."

"Everything is about to change," he agreed with a grin as he set his hand on top of hers.

After they'd celebrated their discovery of the pirate ship with a bottle of champagne and an endless night of lovemaking at Brock's house, their days became consumed by the treasure collection from the pirate ship. The fact that she'd missed her period went over her head until the second month had passed.

They exchanged a delighted smile. "You're going to be the best dad, Brock."

"I don't care whether it's a girl or boy, as long as it has its mother's determination and bravery."

He leaned in to claim her lips in a meaningful way that left her boneless and hungry for more. Pregnancy had made her insatiable. She was even more eager than usual to feel his touch again after exchanging vows while docked in Cannes the evening prior.

She never thought she'd one day have a husband.

Long after her memories returned, she could appreciate the situation she had stumbled into and the fact that she'd accidentally come across the man who was destined to become her soulmate. The treasure that would make them rich beyond their wildest dreams once it was in the hands of the right buyers was an added bonus.

"I love you, Mrs. Resner," he muttered against her lips.

As his fingers brushed along the edge of her bikini top, she moaned in agreement. "I'll love you even more if you take care of this sudden ache I'm experiencing."

As his skilled fingers slipped beneath her top, Beau, the captain they'd hired for their three-month journey through Europe, cleared his throat behind them. He was a soft-spoken man who married an equally soft-spoken Michelin-starred chef who had been hired to prepare their meals while at sea. Normally, Andy adored him. But with the interruption, she had to bite back a slew of curse words.

"Sorry to interrupt, sir and madam." Beau's cheeks reddened as he held out the portable phone. "You have a call from the States...a Miss Squires."

Brock and Andy exchanged a terse look. Four months prior, Knox had been declared dead by the local authorities. To be safe, Andy and Brock hired a woman named Bexley Squires, the most sought-after private investigator on the West Coast, to keep an eye out for him.

While Brock answered the call, Beau caught Andy's eye. "I forgot to tell you, madam…a package arrived right before you and Mr. Resner boarded this morning. There's no return address. It's merely addressed to 'the newlyweds'. I placed it on the master bed."

Andy laughed under her breath. Just hours after the ceremony, they had shared their news with Oswald, Emma, and Skye. She supposed all three of them had the kind of money that would ensure a present would be delivered to a boat docked in France in record time. "Thank you, Beau. I'll come down for it after this call."

Once he stepped away, Brock activated the phone's speaker and set the phone between them.

"…a lead on a man who recently consulted with a plastic surgeon in L.A.," Bexley explained. "I'm not saying he's undoubtedly your guy," she warned, "but this man had similar facial features and bone structure. Plus, he was walking with a limp and a cane that could very well be consistent with a bullet injury."

"Do you know what kind of procedure he was looking for?" Andy asked.

"Yeah, and it's one of the reasons he caught my attention. He said he was an actor looking to change his features for a more traditionally handsome appearance, like Paul Newman and James Dean. My surgeon friend tells me no one in today's show business would request to look like those dinosaurs, especially when they're under forty."

Brock's fingers swept back and forth across Andy's belly. She wasn't sure if he was trying to comfort her or himself, as stroking her belly had become one of his favorite pastimes. "Did you get a picture of the guy?" he asked.

"Already sent it to your email. It's a little grainy since it was a screenshot taken from a security camera, but hopefully, you'll be able to confirm whether or not it's possible this is your former friend." She cleared her throat before lowering her voice. "I'd appreciate it if you'd keep the picture between us. It wasn't exactly procured using standard methods."

"Understood," Brock replied. "How recent was this?"

"Yesterday morning. Last night, I discovered he's hunkering down in an extravagant beach house in Malibu. He signed a rental agreement for the month, so I imagine it's where he's planning to recover after the procedures."

"We just eloped in Cannes," Andy said. "We're on our way to Monaco."

Bexley sucked in a tight breath. "Well then, 'congratulations' to you and your bride. I'd say the chances this Knox character is actively searching for you are probably pretty slim to none, considering he's here and you're living your best life on the other side of the world."

"I hope you're right," Brock huffed, glancing down at Andy's large belly with a loving look. "We have more at stake now."

"You lovebirds relax, enjoy your honeymoon in paradise," Bexley ordered in a more cheerful tone. "I'll keep a close eye on your guy and let you know if there's a valid reason to panic."

"I can finally understand why you're in such high demand," Andy told her. "Thank you for taking us on as clients, Miss Squires."

"It's Bexley. And if you're ever in Papaya Springs, look me up. My husband and I would love to meet you and hear about your adventures. You and the Treasured Ten have become internationally famous."

"It's a date," Brock agreed before ending the call. He tossed the phone aside and leaned in, clearly intending to finally satisfy her urges.

Laughing, Andy dropped a kiss on his cheek before slipping away. "Beau said we received a wedding present while we were in Cannes," she informed him as she slipped a sundress over her shoulders. "Must be from either your sister or Oswald and Emma. I'll be back in a minute."

She waddled—because that's all she could do anymore with all the extra weight she'd put on—down the steps to the cabin. Although they'd merely chartered the luxurious yacht for their trip, she decided they would look into buying one soon. She didn't imagine she would ever tire of living on the water; therefore, they'd need something bigger for when friends and family came to visit. They would also need to hire a nanny and a tutor once the baby was older, and the staff would need separate living quarters.

She was humming to herself as she entered the sleek bedroom surrounded by half a dozen windows showcasing the sapphire-blue waters of the Mediterranean Sea. In the center of the room, the lavish king bed had already been remade since their last round of sex just hours earlier. No matter how many times she told the captain's wife it was unnecessary to dote on them, the woman was apparently obsessed with orderliness.

A large white box with a massive white bow sat at

the edge of the bed. Grinning, Andy released the bow before lifting the top of the box.

Inside was a large white basket filled with baby items—everything from a silver rattle and extra-soft blanket to a stuffed teddy bear and a rubber duck for bath time. Andy plucked the small gift card from its center. The envelope was blank. The card itself was handwritten in a sharp slant Andy found vaguely familiar. Her lips dropped open as she read the words and her belly clenched in fear.

Congratulations on your marriage and the impending arrival of your bundle of joy. Enjoy the feeling of freedom while you can. One day down the road, when your little family is settled into the house of your dreams, know that I'm watching and fully intend to collect on what's rightfully mine.

XOXO, Uncle Knox

On a gasp, Andy dropped the card. Barely a moment later, she felt warm liquid trickle down her legs.

The baby was on its way.

And Knox was watching.

About the Author

With over 45 captivating titles spanning various genres, Quinn Avery first honed her talent for crafting intricate puzzles through her smart and quirky Bexley Squires mystery series. Her contemporary suspense thrillers, often set in her beloved locales such as Mankato and Lake Shetek, are nothing short of addictive, leaving readers spellbound with their mind-spinning twists. When Quinn and her husband aren't off on adventures, they enjoy the tranquility of their Minnesota acreage and lake home in their newfound empty-nest phase.

For more information, visit www.QuinnAvery.com.

Acknowledgments

This book was a long time in the making, as they say. *Too* long. Probably because it ended up being more romantic suspense than adventure, and I unsuccessfully tried fighting the process. As someone who has cherished *The Goonies* since the 5th grade, I just really wanted to write something that involved treasure hunting.

Thank you to my fans and those close to me who put up with the back and forth between the title and cover, especially Najla Qamber and her team, and my dear friend Christy Freeberg. The more dreamy of the two covers/titles won because overall, it fit the theme best.

I wouldn't be the creative person I am today if my dad hadn't introduced me to such epic cinematic adventures as Indiana Jones, Star Wars, and (his favorite) James Bond. Dad, I'll always cherish the memories of seeing those for the first time with you at my side (and mom sleeping on my other side). To be fair, my creativity can also be credited to my mom. Not only did she encourage me to write, she was also known to jot down a poem and short stories when I was little. So thank you, Mom, as well. I hit the lottery in the parental pool! I'm thankful you two passed down your senses of humor as well, or life would be way too boring!